Dark Angel Episode Series

Amy Brown
MS
Psychology

Amy Perez MS

Psychology

Published in 2019

ISBN: 9781092659291

Printed by Amazon

Front Cover Design by Author.

Book Design by Designer.

Author: Amy Perez MS Psychology

https://www.amazon.com/kindle-dbs/author/ref=dbs_P_W_auth?_encoding=UTF8&author=Amy%20Perez%20MS%20Psychology&searchAlias=digital-text&asin=B07H24NKYJ

Episode 1

I had the devil on my side since day one. I just knew it. It was in my blue eyes. When I watched his green skin in the sunlight. Watching it go from black to white just amazed me. As his body curled up on the sidewalk, I knew it was the life for me.

I could be a killer. Why not? There are people out there who need to pay. A ten-year-old burning a frog to death could see that. You fly killing basted. What else could I kill? There was no remorse. No feeling. Did I have a soul? A heart? Did I care about a single person? It was the death of a middle school boy. I didn't even know him. But when I stared into his coffin, I saw the saddest sight of life. A young handsome boy gone.

But why? Why was his life gone? He was only fixing a bike chain. During a high-speed chase, a drunk ass mother fucker killed him on impact. But why? Why him? As I stared at Derek, I wanted to avenge his death.

2

Make people scared and pay. How many times have I fixed my bicycle chain? Why haven't I died? Why is my life worth more than his? As his friends lied Bone Thugs-N-Harmony tapes onto his chest. I saw their pain. I wanted to fall to my knees. To see that kind of grief. All because of some heartless drunk.

But who was I gonna go after? Drunk drivers? Rapists? Murderers? Pedophiles? Who was going to pay for this? Besides? Who was I? God? The Grim Reaper? How was I gonna decide? His death wasn't fair. Someone who has lived a long-fulfilled life was easier to understand. And even that is horribly painful. A ton of people will pay for this. Which is why I had to start with a helpless animal. How could I make a person pay if an animal can't pay? I already accidently killed my hamster. But it was different. There was remorse and pain. Shock. Tears. It was my beloved pet. But then it happened again, and there was less pain. Less care. Why? Where did my remorse go? Where did the pain go? Did my soul leave my body?

3

I didn't even care. I didn't want it back. It was easier that way. To look at death like it was nothing. I roamed the woods for hours. Curiosity burned through me. The fire was uncontrollable. What could I find in these woods in Memphis? The smell of the air is intoxicating. The crunch of the dead leaves is music to my ears. Looking up at the sun beaming through the trees looks like heaven.

I come to a herd of sheep. They are so peaceful. I already passed the no trespassing sign, like always. Even as a young child, I have a passion for breaking the law. Why not? So what if I had a knife on me? Would I slaughter the sheep? I don't like how they are relaxing. Just enjoying life. Life is supposed to be hard, painful. The sheep remind me of the entitled kids at my school. The ones who scoff at me. Sure, I got a couple of play dates. But it was a sympathy act. Here honey, play with the outcast. Whatever assholes. I didn't need their fake kindness.

Just because I liked to watch my Dad gut a fish and roam the woods? Oh yeah and I was a kleptomaniac. I stole from friends and family. But why? Why would a young child do that?

Married parents. Good school. Friends. Was it the molestation? When a much older boy decided to "play house" with me? And my genitals were disrespected. Did my soul disappear when I was hiding in his Mother's closet? Why did that need to happen? Why did I have to pay that price? An innocent child.

4

Molested. I trusted someone who told me to take my shorts and underwear off. Why did he feel the need to do that? As I ran down the street that day, I ran from shame. I left the embarrassment behind. It's not like he was the only one there. There was a room full of children with my naked body exposed. Just to see what the boy who was six years older than me wanted to do. His brother was there, sister and friends. Just another soul stealing moment. Why not? Just take it.

But I was the outcast. Me. Because I still wet the bed? Because my parents were frugal? Because my Dad was big and scary? We had been nothing nice to those people. And that was my payment. As my hair flowed in the wind that day. Something changed. For the bad. The darkness washed over me. Would the light ever return? Back to the woods. Back to discovery. A dead snake. Interesting, he was flattened on the dirt path.

I kneeled down to get a closer look. Did he deserve it? Of course he did. Snakes are bad. They do bad things. Like murderers, molesters and pedophiles. They deserve to be flattened into nothing. Don't they? Would light ever shine through again? What would make me happy? What would make me smile? I don't know. I sit down next to the snake and feel for him. His body is dried and dehydrated. Stepped on? Natural death? What happened to him?

5

I vow to myself that I would make them pay. Molesters and pedophiles. Not now. Because I am small. My arms and legs are skinny. What was a ten-year-old supposed to do? But someday I will get bigger and stronger. I will need help though. I need to build a team. And obviously hunt the bastards down. They are sly and sneaky after all. They hide in popularity. In families. As evil as I feel inside, there is someone more evil than me. A pedophile. Someone who could take a child’s innocence away. But their thoughts will not be castrated. I will work that out with science. But the actions. Why make a child do something that they don't understand?

I want to hunt. I want to see blood. The sheep don't deserve it. And for God's sake, the frog was innocent. I will use my evil for good. But who will walk this road with me? Could anyone else share my monstrous feelings? A ten-year-old's rage? Enough to crack the world in half? I feel the power but no strength. Where is my worth? Was it left in that bedroom? As I lie down next to the snake, I see the sun. And then it falls. One single tear. My innocence. It hits the dirt. Then every single person in Hell falls to their knees. I become their queen. I am gonna make The Black Panther look like Sylvester. Who is gonna be Tweety though?

I let out a scream through the woods. My voice echoes through the trees. Rage goes straight to Heaven and Hell. Cheers and anger ring out from both directions. Even the devil gives up his stance. Jumping up, I hit a tree with my left hand. Right. Left. The pain doesn't even pass the adrenaline. Pure adrenaline masks the blood ripping from my knuckles.

The blood makes me happy. It's my new coping mechanism. Adrenaline. Rage. But not homicidal. More like psychological. I want brains. I rip my tennis shoes off and rip out the laces. I know where I am headed anyways. Into the river they go. Next my socks. I won't need them. I will be barefoot for my people. The victims. And oh yeah, the pedophiles too right? I'm supposed to turn into the monster who bred me right? I will walk through fire for them. Us. I find an anger inside me that will burn forever. Past death.

6

What am I going to do with it? What is going to tame it though? I can't exactly sit down at the dinner table full of rage. So, I bury it.

Deep down inside me. It becomes my tool. My secret weapon. I will use it to my advantage someday. Someday, I will be strong enough to face it. It becomes my first demon. Little do I know; many more will stack upon it. Young and dumb I am. But furious. Full of fire. We all need it. A fire to keep is going. Something to live for. And if need be, die for. Fighting through it will be the only way. It's not like anyone will listen to me anyway.

I'm just a little girl with blonde hair and blue eyes. Hair unkempt. Dirty face and hands. What was the point of molesting me? Why the tomboy? Someone who never "played house" before. Never a tea party. None of it. Why did I let that happen? I willingly took my clothes off. Self-blame is the only way. The only way to survive. Never, ever let it happen again. And the person becomes the snake. Probably worse. I better get to the tiny church down the street from my ranch style home. I will pray for my future forgiveness. Or maybe just sing some Whitney Houston at the top of my lungs on the mic while my Mom cleans that church from top to bottom. That woman works her ass off and guess what? Me too.

Episode 2

15 years Later

1

It was love at first sight. It was like science and romance intertwined. And the sex went to heaven and back. But the interaction was real. The feelings were real. The happy tears. The sad tears. Everything. But what do you with such love? Do you keep it bottled up inside? Do you tell everyone you know? If you have been married to the game as long as me, it would be hard to commit. Never faithful. Never truthful. Everything was always a lie. Until my Dark Angel. He came to me at the darkest moment. I was on my knees. Ready to give up. Throw everything away. But how? How did he just penetrate his light into my life?

It was nothing short of a miracle. How did he see me? What did he see? At first it was the eyes, locking through mine. Then the irresistible smile. The love penetrated through my soul. Terrifying yet exciting. I could never look at him again. The feeling sent me straight to Heaven. I wasn't ready to go yet. His voice moved the depth of my sadness. The crying stopped. I lifted my knees off of the floor. My smile returned. He saved my life a thousand times over. But how? An ocean stood between us.

2

How could a distance bring two people so close? Just one look. One voice. Shattered my earth. The devil refused to take me. God became undecided. Where do these people go who reached too far to heaven? We were punished for being too close before. But why?

A love too strong to separate two souls. Finally, heaven and hell agreed on something. Two people must unite. To save literature, romance, science and divine love. The darkness and the light together forever. As I rode my yellow mustang through the graveyard for answers, my engine woke up every soul. Souls to come with me on my mission. So many answers. What kind of questions would the universe ask? What would someone who ran out of time do? Would they risk everything for love?

Would they swim the ocean? As I drove slowly through the graveyard, I was given a gift. A sixth sense. I became powerful. What did these people want? Resurrection? A second chance at life? Why not. But not in zombie form.

Just a person lost in America. Where do we take the foreigners? Jail? Psych wards? Homeless shelters? The streets? Would they want that? To fight to the top like that? Go through the trenches like me? I raise you a second chance and I up you my utmost protection.

3

As I slowly revved my engine through ancestors, I decided that they were now my people. The winds changed. I was no longer submissive. Dominance raged through my brain. Neurons fired so fast. The card of technology, time and space raped my brain to give me knowledge I never had. Did I pick up more than I bargained for?

What would come to be sacrificed? My life? My first born? Was someone coming to meet me? Time would only tell. But the Dark

Angel decided to protect me. He promised to never let my mind slip into the darkness again. And that promise was kept. With honor. My soul was so corrupt. However, the Dark Angel gave it back. It was in his smile. I just couldn't take it. How do you handle the most beautiful moment of your life? You can't run from it. You can't hide from it. Embracing it feels like a sin. You find balance. A place where you can fight the urges. The thoughts that make one blush and secretly find a place to hide. Where do you put that? You give it to him. Every thought.

Every emotion. The sex. You open yourself in so many ways. Making love is the only option. Kissing passionately as the sun rises. Being in the light together. The imperfections. The happiness just to see the smiles alone. Is the love there? Of course it is.

The ocean becomes a puddle and there is no longer a distance. The only choice is there. The darkness and the light deciding to intertwine and form an everlasting love.

4

The stars align. Fate agrees. Everyone agrees. So why not make it happen? It's the only way. When two souls become one, there is no such thing as separation. If so, the world would shatter. But it would never come to that. Once bodies touch, a decision has to be made. A line gets drawn in the sand and the divine steps in.

Is true love a choice? But how could true love happen? A victim of countless crimes. A woman who has a body count too high to remember. The rage before my murders. The woods became a grave site. No one went there anyways. I always took a break in the winter.

The ground was too hard. I would have gotten caught for sure.

It was so hard to fight the urges. However, it was a great time to research. Study behavior. To think like a pedophile. What would they do in a bathroom? A baseball field? Video games? Where did they find their opportunity? It wasn't until I turned to the internet, gaming and hopping into chat rooms. It was too easy to pretend to be a child. IP addresses became my hit list. My fresh hunting ground.

I found a few friends to help me out. An engineer that wasn't afraid to kill. He kept my secrets. He knew his way around the computer and my heart. Also, my body. The life we created was beautiful. We saved countless lives of children. They got to live in happiness.

Family bike rides, school proms. Countless smiles.

5

I never forgot to visit the funerals of young children and teenagers. I needed the motivation. I needed to see the pain. The tears. After my dignity was ripped from me at ten years old, I decided to make a list and check it twice. However, my grand finale was my predator. He was the head of the FBI.

He resided on A1A. On the soulless road on the ocean. His house, a fortress. I couldn't save the children yet. The whole block was filled with predators like him. Their possessions in protection. Who is going to investigate the investigators? Until I took a rage filled, barefoot walk down the street. Hair down, short dress, no panties.

Lights on everywhere and no one home. Where were the children? I couldn't feel any souls. I sat in front of a halfway constructed building. A new fortress. How many children would end up there? It was scary territory. Making assumptions of people with great power. But why else would someone walk barefoot down an unknown road searching for souls?

I had been speaking with and feeling spirits for days and all of the sudden found silence. There was more to the story. Could I face it on my own? Was it intuition or psychosis? Just staring at the empty building. What if there were pictures of my children in there? What if this was a future abduction sight? I couldn't fight the silence. I closed my eyes for visions. But my brain fought it. I saw chains and blood. It looked like a slaughter house. Then a saw her. A young blonde girl locked in a small cage made for a dog.

6

How could I save her? I already lost God's protection. I tossed my engagement ring in the grass. It was rock bottom. Pedophiles, I will explain. It has part to do with biology and evolution. And of course, psychology. But kidnapping, mangling and murdering was the bottom. Low of lows. I would rather be molested as a young girl and survive. The darkness eventually lifted. Repressed memories played their part. But this? I can't fathom it. There must be a system but could I crack It? Alone? I had to. No one was going to believe me. I would go through the trenches for the lost children. I had to. The industry was too big. The power reached too high. However, the devil and I decided to climb together. Even the devil was pissed. I was calm though. Still sitting. Waiting for a soul. Nothing. Where was everyone? Were they being entertained in chambers down below? Typically, there were no basements in Florida. But power and money can reach levels. Bend laws.

Did they get bored? Then what happened? Tastes changed? Where did this operation start? I needed to know. A police officer circled the block but he wasn't interested in me. What and who was he protecting? Not a young half naked woman. What did I know? As if I couldn't feel the burial ground around me. No sports cars. No RVs. No boats. No rich people toys. Just fortresses. Huge fences. What and who was being protected? Three cop cars rushed to me. My soul searching was over.

Episode 3

1

“Doctor, what topics are we going over today?”

“I'm sorry Gabriella, I am taking a vacation to do some soul searching.”

Gabriella gives a disappointed look.

I didn't think I was that good. I just do a slide show from the textbook.

“I am just going to miss your jokes and funny stories.”

My eyes start to tear up. Sometimes we don't understand how special we are until someone throws it in our face.

“I am so sorry Gabriella, no one can go where I am going.”

Gabriella looks confused.

“I will explain when I get back. Sometimes research can be a lonely place. But it can be necessary to move the world forward.”

“I understand. It is a bit strange, but you are the expert.”

Let's hope so. This could get messy, very messy. I am only going where spirits are.

I have to avenge some deaths. Starting with my first born. I have to do this with no help. I mean none. No person can interfere. Not a friend or relative. These topics are reserved for jail cells, mental hospitals and the divine powers. I am walking a fine line. I have never read the bible. My reading comprehension is too low. I didn't grow up reading books. I only manipulated my environment. It's really all I know. However, I have tasted ashes, been possessed and I can sense when assassins are nearby. However, I have been given a recent gift. A physical litmus test if you will.

2

It came from the souls along with some criminals. Some were wrongly accused. Also, some of my elders are slowly showing up as well. My elders have come to me but I can't use their powers this time. This class has to be taught to the universe first. If I survive during every chapter, through having my sixth sense triggered and raped, I can teach it in the flesh. If not, the deep dark secrets die with me.

Surviving will take every cell in my body and every neuron in my brain. My genetic code will face destruction if my theories are wrong. I have to confess all of my moral sins. If my skull cracks, I lose. The pain in my frontal lobe will be worse than any psychic has ever endured. But like many psychics, I need a place to hide.

Where can I be feared and have my sanity questioned at the same time? Where can the universe decide on me? Where is a place where my death could be painted in a thousand different ways? But why? Why is this the only way? The spirits have to. I agreed to protect a group of people. There are souls that are trapped. No one has gone to bat for them before.

These people may be considered the low of the low. Especially in jail. But at all cost of education, I sacrifice myself on this chopping block. Pedophiles, this your day. Through my body, soul and brain, let's do a spiritual study. It's the least I can do. Why not? I have no financial or social power. My reputation has already been put through every puddle of mud.

I literally have nothing left. Nothing to lose, nothing to gain. But to educate an entire subject of confusion across the world will be worth my life. If one person survives and one child's innocence is preserved, it will be worth it. Every child in the world deserves my path. Children are our future. They must be preserved. I am going through unfamiliar waters to handle such a controversial subject. However, either the water will separate or my sanity will.

3

However, I have done a lot of terrible things that I have hid from the world. However, I have lost one person in my family. My tears are enough to cause a tidal wave. I would never want that. How can I stop the tears? How can I pull myself off of my knees of grief? Use a human survival instinct, think of something worse than losing an elder. Losing a child. That grief would shatter my existence. I would rather be assassinated a thousand times over than have that happen to one more child. Lock me in a cage. Let me trade places with a tortured and mutilated child.

Just give it to me. Just don't let the world crack in half. That is what happens when you are offered the highest sixth sense known to mankind. Every clairvoyant is terrified. Spirits are hiding in places never thought of before. But why? Is it because I enjoy manipulation? Is it my education? Is it my ability to submerge myself in various cultures?

How about being born autistic and never knowing? No one informs me of my mental illnesses. But why? I am done being lied to. I am finished being manipulated. It is my turn now. I get to hide. Protect myself to research that of which baffles the universe. If somebody doesn't like it, too bad. I was chosen. It's not my fault. No one can deny their destiny.

The only people that can and have helped me are my Dark Angels. That's it. The universe sends them every time I try to crack codes. They are my biggest obstacle.

4

Why are they always dressed as my first love? The first person I trusted? The first person I bought a birthday gift for. And my first real kiss. For years, the universe has been playing tricks on me. But now I'm tuned in. I stand at full attention.

I have lied, cheated, murdered and injured people. I have damaged relationships. I have crushed people emotionally. I have walked away from my loved ones. Abandoned friends. I have been fiercely judged. However, I have never judged anyone in my life. I let everyone be themselves.

I don't interfere with biology or evolution. Only when it comes to myself. I am so hard on myself that I have tried and failed at committing suicide multiple times. I am done with that though. Why not let the universe decide? If my sins are the greatest, I will disintegrate to the ground.

If I am not the worst of the worst, I will survive. The people who are terrified of this moment of truth will sit in the shade. The shade or inside a building will be the only place to survive this fateful day. I don't know when it is coming. However, the thought is only known to my spirit. The only one I can’t tap into. I can't read my own mind. I don’t understand my own thoughts or actions. My behavior is ritualistic. I cannot control myself completely.

I leave every thought in my own brain. I only offer small talk, mindless conversation and fake laughter. I never look at anyone in the eyes. I don't even look someone in the eyes when we are making love. I never express my feelings. I keep my theories locked inside of a cage. All I can do is try to pick up various social actions. I never understand the words or actions of others.

5

Human beings make no sense to me at all. I am empathetic to a fault. I can feel energy everywhere. Sometimes the energy is so strong that I have to remove myself.

I get drenched in paranoia the moment I sin. I present myself as fearless, confident and happy. However, I am clumsy, confused and often overwhelmed. I am terrified to make mistakes. God forbid fail. Every time I try something, I fail. Every relationship. Every home. Every job. I am deemed disabled.

Even when I try to prove my sanity, the universe rapes my brain and makes me insane. Now I finally understand why. Powerful people have been fearing my power. So, they have been handing me various mental illnesses my entire life. So much so that they have become my people. I have submerged myself in extreme heat, bathed in ice cold water. Entered places where powerful people fear. My most valuable loved one gave her brain to ECT against her will. My people have been handed lobotomies like Christmas presents. Pedophiles have been chosen as the lowest. That one I can defend. The only three I can't understand are murder, Munchausen and torture. However, these three people hide behind mental illness. Why not? Would someone prefer a mental hospital or jail?

6

Judging by the places I have been, it's a toss-up for me. Innocent people sit in jail while skull crackers, mass murderers and the top Munchausen experts reside in top notch places. But why? I won't put myself in their shoes. Yet. If you were very powerful, you would have nothing to fear. But what if you weren't?

What if you were completely powerless? I have never done anything to become powerful.

So far, the only thing I have done is walk down the street in a dress without a bra and panties. I threw my sandals in the grass and tossed my ring.

But guess what I found? Death row. Death row for innocent victims. But I have to hide? What mental illness is it this time? Anxiety? Depression? Schizophrenia? Every psychiatrist wants to hand me a cocktail of pills and send me on my way. Well guess what? Let's pretend the pills are all placebos. Let my brain do what it does naturally. Let's see who comes to bat for me.

So far, only a few over protective people have shown up. Also, a few guys looking to get laid. But what if I teamed up with murderers, drug dealers, molesters, rapists and even a person who has eaten brains? What if I ruled

Hell for a while? Are my people there? The people with true mental illnesses? If so, I won't be very happy. But if and only if they are there, send me there too. I have a lot of questions. I may be able to grant just one person salvation. Not a stairway to heaven, just a portal. One that they can decide to use or not. Move over Doctor Strange, there is a new doctor in town. No one better blow my cover either.

Episode 4

1

Just like our tears taste like salt from the ocean, we cannot deny that we are tied to the earth and ocean. And just like our world has imperfections, so do we as people. What if I admitted that when I met the second love my life, it was hate at first sight. It was only until I saw his picture as a five-year-old boy with thick glasses and toothless smile, that I fell in love. Does that make me a pedophile? Let's pretend it does. Let me stand before all populations and defend myself. Will I get hung before I finish my speech? Will an assassin wipe me out? Would people groan in disgust? Would I get a standing ovation? There is only one way to find out. How many people march for what they believe in? Justice. Freedom. Equality. How many people have caused an uproar for something they hate? Something they misunderstand.

Do we have to hate each other to protect genetic perfection? Why were the continents separated? Why do people swim oceans at the thought of a better life? Because we can feel it. It's animalistic. We want to give our children the best chance of survival.

2

How did society eradicate certain genetic imperfections? We reproduced across religions, cultures and races. However, we need to preserve the laws of attraction. Some of us love dark eyes. Some of us love dark skin. But why do some of us get sexually aroused and even fall in love with someone much more youthful than us?

This is where biology, evolution and possibly romance make love with each other. Let's just say the earth preserved all girls under eighteen and all men over eighteen. How would society continue? How would we survive as a human race? Would we baffle at the thought of pedophilia then?

Or would that castrated trait go out of the window?

3

What if each group resided on different continents? What if every religious entity from all regions were on their knees begging for forgiveness? What if rape was forgiven? What if abortion was ignored?

What if I was the only one willing to reproducc? Let's pretend that I am twenty-three.

The most attractive guy that I find lives in a different country on a tropical strip of land? However, he is only sixteen. What would the world think of me then?

What happens if him and I kiss? Hit every level of sexuality except the one to reproduce. We know it's wrong. Society taught us that it is a sin. It's wrong. It's disgusting. I can't fight my urges. My motherly instinct kicks it's way in. I am willing to do anything to birth a child. No matter the consequence. No matter the pain. Even if I die.

Women would cross oceans. They would endure extreme heat. They would fight every element to raise my child. What if they were twins? One boy and one girl. We would celebrate. The man I love and I get to marry. No one cares about age anymore. We start to rebuild. Any older boy and younger woman decide to make love.

Society builds new standards. Pedophiles who have suffered and been to unspeakable places have been forgiven.

4

Our ability to be attracted to youth saves humanity. It happens. Even the assassins that were trying to take me out get emotional whiplash. They are laughing, crying and regretting getting paid for my death.

They decide to drop their gun silencers to the floor above my bed and start playing the piano while I make love. They finally agree that some laws in society need to exist they decide to defend me. Laugh with me. Cry with me. Look crazy with me.

However, our continents are divided. Young girls are able to look older with make-up and surgery. Men can use filters to look younger. Who is to blame? Well, technology. Our information is scattered. The system is scrambled. Everyone is confused. What if I see a sexual movie and have no idea that the actors are underage? What if my brain is immature? Is it my fault? I develop a celebrity crush for an underage boy. I fantasize about him. I write him letters.

Become obsessed. Why do I get turned on when I see a baby? It's because I want one. What if I was repulsed? Disgusted. Well, my bloodline would end. However, what if my neurons were misfired, my urges couldn't be controlled. Then it could go the other way. It is a mental illness. A misunderstanding. Do we damn people to hell who get crippled with anxiety? What about someone who is so depressed that they see no light?

What if someone becomes homicidal or suicidal? Do we punish them? No. We don't. We help them. We give them hope. We educate them.

5

So here is some social justice. If someone is sitting in jail for looking at pictures of a person who they weren’t sure of their age and got arrested, then put me in the cell with them. I am coming to save you. I entered an art gallery in Detroit and stared at a lot of nudity. Naked babies. Naked young children along with men and women.

I guess my cell mate and I are on the same page. We are friends. We have something in common. They become my people. At least I get to lock my cell at night. I get to talk about my children. Hang pictures of them in my cell. Damn, they can even come see me. Not bad.

Will I be stabbed in the shower? Raped? Mutilated? Or not because I am a woman? Will younger guys be attracted to me? However, I am terrified to give birth in a prison or a mental hospital. I am extremely scared to give birth without pain medication. If I had to endure the full pain of childbirth, reproduction for me would be off the table.

So, let's all get on our knees and thank the women who have given birth to a child or multiple children naturally. Enduring pain. So many women have died to put a child on this planet. We should give them the highest honor. Not a famous singer. Not a poet or even an artist who painted naked women with their nude children. That is why women march. We are getting educated. Looking at statistics. Finding other paths rather than motherhood.

We are literally handing everyone population control on a silver platter. No one notices. No one thanks us. Some societies have removed support for mothers. We live in isolation with our children. It is lovely yet lonely. But what about the warriors? The women who say fuck it. Decide to keep giving birth until they can't? No matter the cost. They know pedophiles exist. They are aware of rape and murder.

They work to provide for their children while their elders overlook them. Their youth is protected. They are beautiful. Irresistible to men.

6

And how do we treat them? Well the men show respect. They defend them. They honor them. They live and die for them. They see their pain. They see them cry and they cry with them. They hold them all night long. They never cheat on them. They would rather die to prevent their women and children from suffering.

They travel countries to earn money to send food and clothing to their family. They cry themselves to sleep missing their families. Then wake up and work long hours. Risk their lives.

I would rather be molested once than remove this dedication to our women and children. I am not mad at a misfiring of neurons or a confusion. There are too many honorable men to focus on and reward. While never demonizing someone who has an immature brain or can't grasp dates, times and social norms.

I can't stop that from happening. I grew up in ghettos. Moved across the country to a more ghetto place. I walked by houses of murderers, drug dealers and rapists. I had a white apron fill of cash. Snickers in my left and chocolate milk in my right. And of course, a pack of cigarettes and a lighter in my pocket. The city of Miami protected me. They preserved my innocence. Not a person robbed me. Shot me. Raped me.

I walked three miles down a nicely paved sidewalk. With no fear. Why? Because all I saw was palm trees, green grass, tropical plants and animals.

I pray that I wasn't only offered safety because I am white. Because I am not too fond of white privilege. Why? Because all of my angels are dark.

Episode 5

1

"Jasiah, I am sorry, but your girlfriend is in a psychosis."

This can't be reality. My girlfriend is everything to me. I am going to cry for a thousand years. I can't be without her. Why is this happening again? It's all my fault. I took her out of her comfort zone. She has been isolated with the kids for months. I fall to the ground and sob. My body is dead. Take my brain. Take it all. Let me take her place.

How can this be reality? My poor angel. She has been doing everything. Working so hard. My long hours at work. There were so many triggers. I could have helped her. She graduated with honors with a doctorate. She is a psychologist. She was seeing patients. Teaching college classes. Her medicine was working for six years straight. I thought she was invincible. My everything.

2

Rayne, I am so sorry. I failed you. This is all my fault. A dark-skinned Cuban man leans down to my crumpled body.

“Sir, she is in good hands. We have top notch care here. You don’t have to worry.”

How did he reach me? I can't breathe. I can't move. But he was able to reach me. The man lifts up my paralyzed body and sits me in a chair.

My face falls to my hands. Rayne I am so sorry. I am going to lose you forever this time.

The places she has been. The horror she has seen. Is she going to survive this time?

2

"Sir, here is some Coca-Cola and some Lay's potato chips. You need some food before you pass out." An attractive blonde woman hands me the items.

I can't eat. I won't eat until she is better.

"I am sorry I can't take it."

I am hysterical. My frontal lobe is aching. My baby. My everything. Trade places with me please.

"Let me go in with her please!"

"Sir, we can't. We have to get her at a baseline. We are going to take her off of all of her medications and see how she does."

"Take her off all of her meds? She has been taking them for over five years."

"We will have you talk to the doctor in the morning to give you more information."

I can't leave. I need her next to me. Life does not exist for me without her. She is like my air. My sun. My sky. Everything. How do I stay alive? My Apple phone rings. Of course, it's my Mom.

"Hello?"

"Mi Amor, todo estan bein?"

My Mom chokes up in tears. She loves Rayne like a daughter. She is always there for her. This is going to rip her heart out.

3

She is always there for us. She cooks every meal. Works her ass off. But she is older now. Can she really help us this time? With two kids?

The boys are so energetic and cute. She helps my Dad with work because he has a bad back. We are devastated. How can we be going through this again? Thank goodness Rayne is mentally tough. She will push through. She has to. She always does. She will meet us on the other side of the mental pain. Once everyone is asleep, she lets her tears fall like rain. How? Why?

4

“Sir, do you need a ride home?”

Where is my home? I can't go back to our condo. Our pictures are everywhere. Our engagement pictures. Maternity shots. Vacations. The beach. I am dying and I can't stop it. Please let me take her place. Please! How in the hell do I numb this pain?

I can't eat. Drink. I must be her warrior though. Her advocate. I always go to bat for her. No matter what. I pick myself up of the chair. I have to be strong for her.

I walk out of the doors of the mental hospital. I spot her sports car. I will be busting her out of here in it. Soon we will be on the beach together. Right where we got married.

We will make love on the beach. We will be a family. She just has to get better. I grab a 305 cigar. She bought these on A1A to celebrate for some reason. All while blasting rap music.

She is my lover. My best friend. I have to see the light at the end of the tunnel. I must. Just for her. Thank God we have family. They are our backbone so many times in crisis. I don't have to feel as if the whole world is on my shoulders.

She was definitely acting strange and paranoid. She was calling me a murderer and shoving me across the kitchen. She also hadn’t been sleeping for at least three nights.

5

When she is suffering, it can be full swing and hard to reach her. She has to be safe in there. Thank goodness. They separate the women from the men. I don't have to worry about anything. My mind is at ease. I get to visit her tomorrow. My Mom and I can bring the kids.

Rayne will love seeing the boys. She will probably fall to her knees. They are her life. Why do bad things happen to good people? She claims to have a checkered past but many of us do.

She won't even hurt a fly. She literally lets bugs go versus hurting or killing them. I know she has a bad side, we all do. I have lied, cheated, stolen. I have done everything in the book. I would never hurt her though. She is perfect. She's a sunflower.

I light up my cigar and flip the lever to open the top of the car. Should I do something bad tonight? I already lost her for the time being.

6

I need to take the anger out. I need to blow off some steam. What am I supposed to do? Go to Delray? Drive down the highway? Smoke weed? Buy some tequila? Maybe take a cruise down alligator alley. I don't like having freedom thrown at me. She tames me. Tames the beast inside.

Now she can’t save me. Dammit. No Jasiah, you can do this. You are stronger than this. I'm sorry my baby, I have failed you. This is the last time I swear.

I fire up the engine and it roars through the night. I will let the stars guide me. Rayne always does it. How does she do it? She better not get hurt in there. Sometimes she enters those places like a firecracker. Other times it's deep depression.

She is probably going to get Haldol though. My poor baby. I love you with all of my heart and soul. Please show your good side in there. Get stable as soon as possible. The Universe needs you.

Episode 6

1

"Jolene, how could you lie to Jasiah and tell him I'm staying in a hospital?"

"I had to my love. I wanted to get some time alone with you. Plus, The Nerds need you."

Damn, this must be serious. I knew it. They have been picking my brain like crazy. They are searching for the Easter eggs in my story. They don't understand. Those are for their protection.

"Rayne, people are trying to possess you, I am here to save you."

"How could you know about that?"

"Rayne, it took us a while to catch up but we have been picking apart your occipital lobe. Storing your memories for you."

It all makes sense now. I never get headaches and now all of the sudden, they are non-stop.

"We typically do it at night but we weren't getting enough information."

I look at Jolene confused.

"You need us. When you are sleeping, all we see are happy memories and some sexual fantasies."

"Well, that's embarrassing, is this necessary Jolene?"

"Yes, it is Rayne. Jasiah is forcing us to go through every closed door that you have and there are many. It's just that with your knowledge and experience, it will put you through the ringer."

"Okay Jolene, I understand."

"First, you must pay the universe the ultimate price."

"And that is?"

"We will need a cure from you."

"Anything Jolene."

Jolene pulls in for a romantic kiss.

"I love you Rayne."

"Jolene, I love you with all of my heart."

Passionate kissing rips through us like the tides of the ocean. We feel the energy from each other and breath life back and forth. The urges are too strong and our lips are too soft.

The universe says yes to our connection. But will Jasiah?

2

Jasiah has to approve of us being together for it to last. But for now, our connection is with each other. No one else. We can touch and kiss all night long.

This bedroom belongs to us and only us. Everything will be shared between us. Soft kissing and touching isn't enough. We need more. Our bodies are aching and calling for each other.

Small talk isn't enough anymore. No more awkward glances. Making love is the only option.

"Rayne, you are my everything. Since the day I saw you, I knew I needed you. I want you in my life forever."

Jolene stands up and strips down to her panties. I follow suit. Tonight, we become one as two women of the sun. The moon agrees and the stars align.

3

The morning sun rips across my face. I see pale skin and pink lips. An angel right before me. We share something so special and sweet. I caress Jolene's gorgeous body. She is flawless from head to toe. I want more of her but I want to let her sleep.

I cannot wait for our deep discussions over breakfast. Just to look in her crystal eyes.

Sometimes I see pain. Sometimes rage. But most of the time it's love. Love for me. My family.

She loves everyone and everything. Not everyone sees it. Not everyone feels it. But I do. I slowly kiss her forehead. I cover her up to her waist in a soft blanket. I caress her breasts. I love her. I stand up and slip on my dress. No panties, just how she likes it. That's what you do when you love someone. You may have to do something different or out of your ordinary.

I step out of the bedroom and slightly close the door. I sneak out on the balcony. I hate to go behind her back but I have to report to my headquarters. After I entered the hospital, I encountered an injection. I am not allowed to know what it is. I must simply survive through it.

I am being studied. Jolene has no idea. It would crush her if she knew that I was silently dying. It could be a lethal injection or a cure. Or both. Only the researchers know. This is only one part of being an agent. There is also a lot of fun and laughter. But right now, I am doing field work. All while living a sense of normalcy.

Jolene and I have been this way for a while. I don’t think anything will change anytime soon. I literally fantasize about her all of the time. I am totally in love. All while uploading my symptoms in a database.

I hope my network is secure this time. Last time one's work got leaked and it caused an uproar and panic. It's hard when your brain gets warped. It's all part of a day's work. As I wrap up my survey, I know I am doing something good. I am helping. I will donate my blood when it is time. My DNA will be replicated and distributed accordingly. Depending on which hospital I enter, I will know or be instructed on what is needed.

I feel small soft hands wrap around my small waist. Chills go up my spine. Sweet kisses go down my neck. Jolene. I lean back into her and put my hands on her hips. I can tell by her body language that last night wasn't enough.

4

Jolene grabs my hand to lead me back to the bedroom. I will let her be the dominant one. For now. She has some gifts. Also, some gifts laying out for us on the bed. Along with a blind fold. I drop to my knees submissive to Jolene. I pull her panties to the side and taste her.

It's never enough. She is sweet and heavenly. She owns me and she knows it. She pulls at my hair and moans deeply. How can we even stay away from each other? I feel my sight go as the blind fold is wrapped around my eyes. I see Jasiah. He would definitely enjoy this but Jolene wants me all to herself.

She leads me over to the bed. I lie down slowly because I have no idea what to expect. She has me in a trance. She rains over me in so many ways. Sexually is only a small fraction.

Jolene grabs my hands to tie them to the bed frame. I am yours Jolene. Take me please! Soft hands caress up my thigh. Up and down as soft as can be. Instant vibration between my legs. I can't stop it. I can't fight it. I want to reach out and touch her but I can't. I want to taste her but I can't. I have to be patient.

She has to have her way with me. It's a loving and luxurious process.

5

"Jolene….?"

"Yes my love?"

But I have no words. She is too much. My body is at full attention. I need her but I am reluctant. It's hard to surrender yourself to someone in this way. Her lips start at my ankles and work their way up my legs. I wasn't expecting this. She always starts at the lips. She wants me to pay. Suffer.

"Jolene?...."

"Shhhh…"

But I want to beg her. She has me where she wants me. Dripping for her. Oh my goodness. I can't take it. She is too hot. She is too much for me. How did I get her? How is she into me? She is too good for me. Above me. Every time. I will never understand it. I'm feeling soft vibrations.

My legs are shaking. Imagining her slight smile. Then I hear footsteps slowly walk away. Hmmm…. this is new. Where could she be going?

"Jolene?" I cry out.

But nothing. I always trust her with this. But now? I am turned on but scared at the same time. I already had trust issues to begin with. She knows this. I was always afraid that this could happen. Being tied up and alone.

I hear the shower turn on. Oh Jolene. Why would you taunt me like this? You know I want you. All of you. But I can't escape. So now I am left here just fantasizing about her. She knows what she is doing. And I love her.

All of the sudden, I hear knocking at the front door. Curiosity stretches through my body. So unexpected.

“Who's there?” I cry out.

The doorknob twists open. The door swings open. Why Jolene? Why? I hear boots hit the tile floor.

6

Jolene, please come out of the shower. I'm sorry. I'm so sorry. Whatever I did, please forgive me. I love you. I really do. I don't mean to live a double life. I want everyone to know about us. I really do. I hear the sink running in the kitchen.

Jolene, please hurry. I feel a sense of urgency to escape but I can't.

Oh Jolene.

I hear humming from the shower. Jolene’s sweet voice.

I'm so in love with her. Whatever her plan is, I'm okay with it. The door cracks open to the bedroom. Who on earth is at the door? Footsteps go through the carpet. Hundred and fifty pounds?

I'm scared. So confused. I'm exposed but not as worried about that. I feel protective. Take me. Save Jolene. Take me instead of her.

She's innocent.

Episode 7

1

"This isn't exactly what we pay you for Rayne."

Embarrassment flushes my face. I'm wishing it was my boss. But no. It's my boss's boss. He's untouchable. He can literally do whatever he wants. For all I know, him and Jolene are sleeping together. He's manipulative and he's good. And honestly, not bad looking.

"Max, I'm…."

I feel rough hands untying me. Then I feel clothes thrown at my stomach.

Work clothes. Not my favorite uniform. The risky hazardous warfare one.

"I have your boots too."

Of course you do.

"There are dogs out for this one so good luck girl."

It is kind of like a game. If the dogs sniff you out, you get to sit in quarantine. And the quarantine operation is well brutal. You are lucky to come out in one piece or at all. This is the price I pay for not watching the news.

I definitely have something going on. I woke up in the unit covered in fluids. I keep having flashbacks of an elder helping me in the shower. One of my newest dark angels. She always has my back. She treated me with such respect. And most importantly, she always helped me find my way home.

Our elders are so important. Grandparents, great grandparents. They see more than we could ever begin to. They pray for us. They cry for us. And even though they don't admit it sometimes, they need us.

2

This past stay in the lab, I was relying on all of the technicians on staff. Sometimes I get the most invasive and newest treatment. It must be my young and fun-loving nature. This time, I overheard something about biotechnology. The pills I swallowed did have a metal component at each end. I've been feeling weird pains in my organs at different times.

My ovaries have been in a lot of pain. Hopefully it isn't pregnancy. Giving birth to an AI baby is very difficult. Jolene would know. She is the first AI baby to be born. Thank God the general public doesn’t know about it. It could cause a lot of warfare trying to get her.

Also, she knows a lot of secrets. For instance, there are more planets than we are taught about in school.

When I landed here in Delaware, it was like I couldn't even breath the air properly. When I fall asleep on the jet, I never know how long I sleep. My team loves to prank me. I could end up anywhere.

Let's see if Rayne can guess what state she is actually in or of she is on the same planet. If someone gives me a needle during flight, I could be out for hours or days. I can't even pretend to be mad. I honestly love it.

When my brain is being toyed with or manipulated, it is like psychological sex for me. I sort of coined the phrase with my team. We have completed psychological sex a few times. However, we are still trying to figure out how it works. It was my job to try and figure it out for a while. It is part of our human race evolving.

3

People could literally have a sexual encounter through the mind and technically be satisfied. It was interesting to play with. Especially when an entire group was involved. I even ended up with a very passionate kiss at the end.

I loved every minute of it. But I am with Jasiah. If Jasiah finds out about the kiss, well I won't have to worry about not being able to breath on another planet. He takes his obsession with me to another level. He is so talented that it's scary. Also, he has many magic powers. He can mind read and mind bend. He is actually considered one of the most powerful witches from the New Orleans area.

He often visits there to renew and upgrade his powers. I tried to explain how people could literally make love through the psyche and he damn near lost his mind. He pulled out my favorite kitchen knife when it turned into an argument. He swore that the elders would be honored to sacrifice me for the greater good.

The greater good only serves the earth, heaven and hell. I answer to the universe. Our cause is completely different. His solutions can be very carnal and sometimes inhumane. It's like the witch community has to end someone over a mistake or two. Which is understandable if it were in the nineteen hundreds. However, we are in the two thousands. Life is so long. We are on the verge of living for two hundred years. That is a long time to live mistake free.

Which is why a lot of my work is spent understanding the why's of human behavior. Why would someone rape? Murder? Steal? It is my life's work. The universe doesn't love it. My boss Steve says to leave that cause to someone else.

"You are above that," he says.

He thinks my brain capacity is too large for it.

"Rayne, your neurons are expanding faster than normal."

I can still see the look on Steve's face. The look of love and fear. We have worked together for a long time. Our conversations go from religion to science to our passions and it's beautiful. We have a deep level of connection on the conversational level. His intelligence is unmatched. Which is why the night we made passionate love I wasn't surprised.

4

Steve knew what my body needed. It's like he could read deep down in my mind and he put his hands right where I needed them. When you are with an AI, it is sex. With a human, it is making love. Humans have a soul. Emotions. I do love Jolene but she just will never be human. She isn't exactly a robot but she is far from human.

When I look in her eyes, I just don't see a soul. It bothers me. Also, she collects data like a computer. Also, she has cameras as eyes. And in today's world, you don't know who has camera lenses or glasses or not. If someone is looking your way, you could be on any channel. Which is why Jasiah will only make love with the lights off. He is such a gentleman with me. But I want to see him. I want to look deep into his eyes.

I feel him in many ways, I really do. I feel like he is always watching me. He has a lot of people. On top of that, he and his family can shapeshift. Which I only recently learned. How could I be with Jasiah for ten years and never know this?

How long has he and his family been watching me? Following me? Is our relationship genuine or was it a set up? When we met in New Orleans, it's like Jasiah had me in a trance. Even from day one, he always tries to go through my phone.

5

I keep trying to explain to him that I can't let anyone go through my phone. Jasiah seems very angry about it.

“I'm sorry Jasiah.”

I could sense the feeling of control back then but I welcomed it. There was just something about it that I fell in love with. As if someone was protective over me. As I met everyone in his family one by one, I realized that they are very special. I wasn’t alone in the universe any longer. I sensed that I belonged to a tribe or a divine group.

Even with that, I just can't marry Jasiah. There is something about him. I love him I just don't want to have a sense of control over him. I want him to be independent. I don't think that he should only be with me. But he begs to differ. He pushed his way into my life.

6

I pull on my black jeans and my white tank top. Max forgot my bra. I walk out towards the door. My brown boots await me. My feet are destroyed from my five mile walk from the airport to surprise Jolene. I also have some weird bumps from running barefoot in Mexico.

"Here, you will need these."

Max hands me some thick white socks.

"I hope you showered good Rayne."

"Of course I did," I lie.

Panic starts to take over my body. If we get too far into an infection and it takes over our body, we are not spared. Not everyone knows that we get infinite lives.

However, God can step in and have us "sleep" for a while. Also, reincarnation is an option.

I open the front door. I wasn't planning on leaving Jolene until the end of the week. She has a lot of pull with many people and the technology world. Max and I sneak out of the front door. Goodbye Jolene, I love you I really do. I'm just not in control.

Episode 8

1

"It's Polio." Max looks at me with concern.

His black Hummer with tinted windows awaits us in front of Jolene's apartment complex.

"Excuse me?"

"Rayne, we are counting on you. Don't blow this."

I breath in deep, wait three seconds and exhale slowly. Now I see why they were teaching anger management classes. It saved Max from getting a nice slap.

"I have children!"

"Rayne, you have the best track record. Your immune system is the strongest on the team."

I love being part of the greater good. But now I have to basically live in solitude without my family. Not my favorite way to work. Looks like I will be looking for a one bedroom in the city somewhere. Good thing my only physical contact was basically with a robot. Dammit! I went through a fucking airport with this shit!

Sat on a plane for three hours. No wonder I felt inclined to walk to Jolene's place. Us humans, we have an intuition. My intuition could be skewed because of my PTSD. You enter the war with a clear brain and what you get is well a surprise. I need a bullet list for my symptoms.

2

Somehow, miraculously, I am able to stay stable. However, if the voices get too loud or I can't sleep for more than two days, I have to check in. We get treated but we have to pay a price. It's a win for the units and hospitals. It's basically free research for them.

I can't complain because I will need medication adjustments for my entire life. However long that will be. I honestly feel like I hit a windfall because I get to live a life of purpose. I can secretly save many lives and consequently, my own. I live entirely off the grid. No contact with distant family members. Staged social media accounts.

As far as anyone is concerned, I am an employee at a makeup store and I hang out cooking and cleaning all day. Also, I hang out with my kids all day and night. It sounds pretty ideal right about now. I mean Polio?

"Max, wasn't this disease eradicated?"

"Yes, on earth."

Oh dear God. No. I don't even like flying across the United States much less the galaxy. My kids have done more space travel through school than I have.

"So, let me get this straight," I stammer out.

"I'm ready," Max rolls his eyes at me.

He never takes me seriously. Like my feelings don't matter at all. Max is always so calm and ready for anything.

"Where am I supposed to put you?!"

Max's face turns from relaxed to upset. If it wasn't for his dark complexion, I would see a face of red. I've never seen him angry.

3

He was on my unit this time. Flashing smiles. He is very handsome. And Tall. Tall, dark and handsome as they say. I keep having a flashback of him grabbing my foot while I was asleep and I wake up to see him standing over me smiling. Was it really him? Or was I hallucinating? That is bad to bring up now I assume.

“I'm sorry?”

Max doesn't say anything. He doesn't need to. He's disappointed in me. I was only supposed to be Jolene's friend. Teach her to do girlie things. Go shopping. Do yoga.

"We tried Max; we really did."

Why didn't you say you were bisexual?"

Now I'm fucking pissed.

"There wasn't exactly a box to check on my application to the service."

"Really?"

"Really, Max what is the real problem?"

"You Rayne."

This asshole is really testing me. Max locks the doors and puts on the safety locks. Damn, he's good. He knows me too well. I have a good track record for running from my problems.

"You can't run from your own brain young lady."

I make sure to give a big eye roll and sigh.

"No shit."

"But you seem to think otherwise."

I am notorious for walking away during a fight or confrontation. I always thought it was the best to not fight. I think times have changed though. You can't just lose your mind and walk away.

It creates too much unnecessary chaos.

"We had state troopers looking for you missy."

A feeling of nausea washes over me. Just so I could surprise my girlfriend.

"So, I'm not allowed to do a surprise visit ever?"

"Not at the moment Rayne, not while the virus is live. You are building antibodies."

"Well that's good to know. Nanotech?"

"Uh you could say that Rayne. Do you keep up with technology at all?"

I bow my head. It's a topic way over my head.

"Rayne, you are lucky to still be in control of your own body with what's running through your veins.

4

"Well that explains a lot. I feel like my body is being probed at."

"Rayne, some very rich and powerful people bought their way into your body via micro technology in those pills you were taking."

"Why am I not surprised?"

"So for the next month, there will literally be an internal war inside you."

"Interesting."

"I know we have a plastic surgeon, a disease specialist, a few higher ups in the air force as well as a few members of the black market."

"How could you?"

Max holds up a hand in defense.

"Not me."

I look at Max Puzzled.

"Do you remember donating your body to science in the state of Mississippi?"

Oh my. Okay that. I was just a young college girl when I did that. A factor of being young and dumb.

That was before I knew that I would be granted eternal life by joining the service. And that my family would too by me joining the secret service. How was I supposed to know that we have multiple Gods, Devils and Jesus's? Who in their right mind would ever think that? I was so naïve back then. I figured I could die at any age.

I figured well, use my dead body to further research and help mankind for the future. I never thought that I would be doing it in the flesh. I am always testing new pills and injections. Some people may think that I have a problem with it, but I love it. I really don't mind. As long as the checks keep rolling in to feed my family, I don't mind.

5

I would do anything to take care of my family. I push further, work harder and try more. Just for Jasiah and my children. I am also motivated if I am helping any child honestly. They are our future. Our forever. They are the ones who become doctors, lawyers, researchers and teachers.

We need their fresh eyes to move forward. To evolve. This world is so big and scary. Every day I am mind blown by our new advancements and discoveries. What is in the future for my children and I?

I am so sick of only being able to see them through a screen. I want them close to me. I want to be able to hug them and tell them that I love them. I want to have a boxing match in the kitchen the way we always did. I want to leap in the pool while we splash each other and laugh.

Those boys are my world. I just hope that the universe knows it. I can only hope and pray I get to see them soon. I know that they are in good hands. Jasiah's family is beyond amazing. I know that they are teaching them to break boundaries. Jump higher and run longer. Only time will tell if they are more from their gene pool, my gene pool or a hybrid.

6

Jasiah and his family are shape shifters after all. My heritage is a secret. I'm trying to hide it as much as I can. Thousands of years ago, we could only come out at night. However, genetic evolution solved that problem. I think I might be devolving though. I no longer want food like I used to. I literally can't stand the taste.

Also, I only want drinks that are red or blue. Orange is okay too. I can't figure out what is wrong with me. I should have gone to my elders with this problem. The one I needed to talk to is no longer around. I feel his energy but I can't actually speak to him. The depression pain from losing him is almost too much to take.

Max slams on the breaks. What the hell? Max takes out a syringe full of white liquid and pierces a needle through my thigh.

“I'm sorry Rayne.”

Episode 9

1

"Rayne? Rayne? It's me, Jasiah."

I slowly open my eyes. I feel like I am coming down from a huge hangover. I grab the side of Jasiah's face. He stares at me with love and care. He is always there for me no matter what.

I was starting to doubt our relationship after everything I've done and have been through. I just can't believe his loyalty. Does he know about Jolene? The Polio? Jasiah strokes my hair. I look around to see a few guys from my unit. They are wearing gear from the local college.

It's safe here. I will be okay. Max left me in a good place. I must trust the process. Where did he go anyway? Did I dream all of that?

“The boys?”

“It's okay, they are safe.”

That's all I need to know. If I know too much, it could be damaging. Enemies can use our most valued loved ones against us.

“Why didn't you tell me?”

Panic washes over me. Which lie was Jasiah exposed to? This could bad. Very bad.

“What on earth are you talking about?”

I sound like I'm half drunk. I supposedly am not allowed to drink anymore. Or smoke. God forbid I have a cup of coffee. Everyone wants to control my life and tell me what to do.

I'm so over it. Jasiah and I have been fighting a lot. When we fight, he has his family take over with the boys and he brings me here. I am becoming the laughing stock of the agency. The guys were poking fun at me for being dropped off like a disobedient dog. Whatever.

2

As far as Jasiah is concerned, it's my PTSD acting up and that this is merely a plain hospital. Jasiah doesn't need to know exactly what I do. Especially in here. Could I pass him polio from being this close? I should have paid better attention in that biohazard seminar. Max and I were passing glances and he was rolling his eyes. He is my most recent dark angel. He keeps my spirits up. He also gets me out of jams left and right.

Our messages are passed in an encrypted app on our phones. However, when Jasiah drops me off here, I don't get to have my phone or any personal items besides clothing.

All of my privacy gets violated. I recently noticed some of my messages getting opened before getting able to read them. So, it's either Jasiah being nosey or someone is really good at hacking.

We recently had a seminar on cyber security. Although I can't believe it, people can access the front facing camera. Also, the back one. Terrorists are using the hack to spy on agents. Even some Instagram models are being targeted. We are being told to cover our cameras with a special sticker so I obliged.

3

When Jasiah saw the stickers, he lost his mind. He was saying I was being paranoid. And yet again, he brought me to the "hospital." And yet again, I was getting laughed at. Every time Jasiah called to check on me, the technicians had a blast making up stories about what kind of things I was up to.

At least I actually have a mental illness brought up from my past. Molestation takes a toll on my brain. Nightmares and paranoia are only the beginning. I have seen agents fake a mental illness their whole life. It makes mental hospitals the perfect place for us to meet up and do our work. We only have to be present for visiting hours.

This hospital only has visiting hours on Tuesday evenings and Saturday mornings. We can get a lot of work done in the meantime.

When I first arrived here, it was technically supposed to be women on one side and men on the other with locked doors in between. It made Jasiah happy to hear. But once I got upstairs, there were a group of men using bedrooms at the end of my unit.

The men had dark hair and tan skin and were being guarded by men in uniform. I wanted to be informed and briefed on what was going on. But if it isn't your mission, you are not allowed ask questions. I have grown to let a lot of things slide. It does make it hard to sleep at night. It seems like someone could just sneak into your room and wipe you out. We don't know if some of the "patients" are simply patients, criminals or agents. Also, they could work for the hospital. It makes it very fun and scary.

"Why didn't you tell me you are pregnant Rayne?"

How and the hell could I be pregnant? Oh my. How am I going to explain this? I am not really pregnant. Last week, my colleagues and I wanted to do a little experiment. We trimmed a half an inch off of our hair and mixed it with a solution. Then all at once, we swallowed it.

4

According to an ancient legend, we can pass immunity that way. Also, we wanted to see how it would show up on a blood test. Looks like our little experiment came back to bite me in the ass. Max and his supervisor approved it. Did they set me up? The technicians do love to take turns making up stories about me to Jasiah. And they are really good.

“I'm not pregnant baby.”

Jasiah gives me a long hopeful stare.

“The doctor emailed me a copy of your urine test. Your HCG levels are off the charts.”

Okay so we tested our blood to see that our DNA was altered but we didn't examine our urine. How could we be so stupid? We even did a swab of saliva before and after.

“Well that's great my baby! I'm so excited!”

Jasiah hugs me and squeezes me extra tight.

“This is amazing!”

I hide my blank expression while my face is in Jasiah's shoulder. I'm not too excited yet.

While this could possibly be true, something tells me it's a false positive.

But what if it's true? I already have two children. Can I handle a third? Jasiah loves babies. We would have ten children if it were up to him. I feel like we got lucky with two healthy boys. Why chance it? I'm not going to ruin his moment. Then it dawns on me. My face immediately flushes. The micro technology.

5

Could they possibly inseminate someone via a computer? I've heard rumors of immoral experimentation on a lot of mental health patients down in the city. What did the technician say? Oh yeah, the more out of it, the better. This is not good for me. The child could be an AI. I don't think Jasiah and his family will be ready.

But my family would be. Is that why Max was questioning me about possibly moving out West? There are so many technology companies that we call it the technology region. Drones deliver everything from a pizza to medicine. All of the housewives have robots cleaning their homes and tending to their children. I don't want that life. I like to get down and get my hands dirty. Just like Jasiah's family.

The first thing my parents do with my boys is hook them up to virtual reality. My youngest went back to school swearing that dinosaurs are real and that he pet one. Virtual reality has come a long way since it first came out. There are cheap headsets that you can buy off of the shelves.

My parents have the real deal. It triggers all of the senses. Sight, smell, hearing, touch and taste. Last time I was out West, people literally weren't even eating. The dining experience was done completely in a virtual reality setting. Wine, dinner, dessert, everything. It just doesn't make sense to me.

6

People were bragging about not having to use the bathroom anymore. That was the worst dinner party of my life. Especially when my parents caught me smoking weed with the kitchen staff on the balcony of their friend's mansion. My Dad ripped the joint from my hand and warned that I could be fined or even arrested. There is zero tolerance against smoke of any kind there.

Vaping is slowly becoming illegal there too. The entire West is ran off of solar power and wind energy. Big secret, I get to live forever so I'm not too impressed. God forbid I have a smoke and some fast food. Well, now that I could possibly be a vessel for a tiny human, I will have to be as healthy as I can be. Now I'm wondering what is going to happen.

Once I've ever become pregnant, I felt so vulnerable and afraid. What if I become unable to work? What if I get put on bedrest? This could be a blessing or a curse.

"The doctor said that based on your hormone levels, there could be multiple babies."

"Really?"

Tears fill my eyes. Tears of joy, surprise and fear. I need to talk to Max. I'd like to see how the gentlemen involved with the nanotech feel or if they are in charge of this.

Episode 10

1

This definitely has to be a mistake. With science now, these results could be from anything. Plus, my doctor could have a hidden agenda. I mean, how long can nanotech last in your system?

"Baby, I have to go. I will see you on Saturday."

Jasiah and I share a passionate kiss.

"I love you Jasiah, give the boys a kiss for me."

"I will."

Jasiah walks out of a back door. In walks a young attractive woman in her twenties towards me. She has red hair and greenish-blue eyes. She smiles and stumbles a bit. She looks like she could almost pass for a child.

"Hi, are you Rayne?"

"Who's asking?"

I don't know this girl or where she is coming from.

"Baylor and Braxton sent me in here to talk to you."

"Oh yeah?"

"Your oldest has been part of The Nerds for a while."

I am totally not surprised. That boy knows computers inside and out. Sure, he is nine years old. Him and I have played video games since he was three. Now that he is getting older, I am less and less in control. I taught him as much as I could. I tried to give him a good moral compass.

"He is climbing up the ladder very quickly."

"Oh really?"

This could be bad.

2

Some of the highest members of The Nerds are some of the best hackers in the world. Baylor seemed to hack into my bank accounts when he was in first grade pretty easily. Lord knows what he is into now. The Nerds spans across the entire world. The members hide behind gamer handles, chat rooms, online schools and even the dark web. They work towards the greater good. Protecting children and innocent people.

"We are involved in the nanotech you ingested."

A laugh escapes me.

"Are you okay?"

"Yes, I am perfectly fine."

I should have known. For days, every time I would close my eyes, I would literally see video games being played. I seriously thought I was going off the deep end for sure. But it was Baylor and his friends trying to reach me. I've been having visuals of everything from Sonic to Roblox to visions of games I have never seen before.

They must have access to my occipital lobe and possibly my retina. I am fully intrigued and want to know more. Unfortunately, now that

I am getting experimented on, I don't always know what is going on.

"We are tracking a disease specialist named Dr. Calvin. He doesn't have good intentions. He is literally digitally passing the genetic code to viruses that we have never seen before."

"Oh."

I start feeling sick to my stomach.

"Your boys are fighting day and night to stop him."

My eyes fill up with tears. They were never supposed to get involved. I still see them as young and innocent. Hell, they are young and innocent. I'm in shock. They are going to bat for me.

3

“I'm sorry what was your name again?”

“I go by Nature Number Three.”

“I will never forget that.”

“Baylor and Braxton said that you wouldn't.”

How is this possible? That is an inside name between the boys and I. I hope that they really trust her.

“I am not an AI but my parents have been replacing my body parts one by one since I was five.”

“That's interesting.”

You never know what to believe and what not to believe in these places.

“Do you want to go to the cafeteria and get a drink?” I motion for Nature to follow me.

“Do you have psychological blood?”

My ears perk up. Looks like this girl knows a lot more about me than I thought. That was something from a lecture I taught a few years back.

“How do you know about that?”

“I've spoken to a few of your students, why are you taking a break from teaching?”

“I am moving on to move on to bigger things I say sarcastically.”

Nature looks at me with empathy and also as though I am a bit pathetic.

“Rumor has it, your PTSD is taking over.”

A big smile crosses my face. Max. He is way too good at his job. My PTSD is nowhere near extreme. I've roomed with people who are much worse off than me. Veterans, human trafficking victims, not to mention the people who were the first to colonize Mars and manned the space missions.

The stories I hear are almost unbelievable. The survivors of the Vietnam war are the saddest. Also, the victims from the border patrol issues from the early two thousands. But what doesn't kill you makes you stronger right? The United States created a savings account for health upgrades for everyone back in 2030. Depending on the hardship and medical issues, the accounts can get pretty high.

War Veterans received hundreds of thousands of dollars. I was beyond ecstatic when the bill got passed. Not everyone was though. Many religious groups didn't believe in the money being granted. Even more so, the medical advances. Companies started printing 3D hearts like they were newspapers.

4

Scientists and doctors finally had something to live for. And in some cases, die for. Some experimentation centers were getting destroyed. It was the first time in forever that our country was more concerned about what was going on within its borders than beyond. Many foreign governments and companies wanted to get involved in selling medical supplies to America. Everyone wanted a piece of the pie. There was such a windfall for the broken and injured Americans.

People would have to do a lot of research into companies before agreeing to certain operations or as we call them upgrades. Groups of people would picket and riot in the streets.

They were claiming that citizens were using tax payer dollars for plastic surgery.

I try to stay positive and see the bright side. While it was hard, it helped advanced our future. Doctors, scientists, developers, engineers and even lawyers got so much experience; it works like clockwork now. Many new college courses emerged. Anatomy and physiology books had to be completely rewritten. Our ways of living got turned upside down.

Even the criminal justice system's boat got rocked. People were practically turning themselves into super heroes within a week's time. Not everyone exactly used their powers for good. Judges who sat for years were throwing their hands up not knowing how to punish people. Life in prison took on a whole new meaning. Especially when some criminals could break down the walls of the prison with a few punches with a metal enforced arm.

I certainly never planned for this. When I was a teen Mom, I never saw any if this coming. I was so busy working and going to school that I didn't have time to keep up with the media every step. I mainly paid attention to the advancements in psychology and sociology. I had one goal since ninth grade and that was to graduate with a doctorate in psychology.

5

Also, I wanted to join the service. I'm a perfect fit for them because of my PTSD. Just check in for a bit to the hospital and perform my missions. Also, I teach and provide therapy as my civilian job. It's the best. I never wanted the boys to get involved. Who knows how much Jasiah knows at this point.

Growing up the way I did makes me protective and literally paranoid. But on the outside, I look calm and collected. I leave the freaking out to Jasiah. He really is the best. If he knows about the service, he might walk away. Or ask me to choose. Max says that my mental behavior is a perfect cover for me.

He claims if I start sharing secrets or talking about the service, Jasiah will just ignore it. He tells me to remain the desperate girlfriend waiting for my white, magical wedding. I hate it because I can't share my real knowledge. I have to play dumb. Thank goodness for Max. He allows me to have my intelligent conversations. We can share our secrets and other information.

"Rayne?"

"Yes Nature?"

“That isn't the only battle you are fighting.”

I think I know where this is heading. I wish my children didn't know what was going on. These issues are definitely too advanced for them.

“A team if clairvoyants got wind of what is going on. They are huge feminists and they feel like what you are going through is wrong.”

“What do I tell them?”

All of the sudden a team of agents enter the backdoor with guns drawn led by Max. Is this for me or Nature?

Episode 11

1

"Both of you, put your hands up!" Max yells out in a serious authoritative tone.

"Especially you Nature."

I hear a loud thud on the roof of the building. What or who in the hell was that? With all of these medical upgrades, you never know.

Nature looks at me with a big smile, "I hope you are up for a little traveling Ms. Rayne."

The ceiling breaks through in the middle of us. I'm waiting for gunfire from Max's end but there isn't any.

"Rayne no!" Max jolts and runs towards me.

Nature 3 and I are grabbed and pulled by three men in uniform. We are greeted by some characters in a plane that looks more like a spaceship.

"Let's move!" Nature yells to her team.

The vessel we are in encloses and rips through the sky. I really hope I am back for the next visiting hours or that this doesn't end up in an uproar. I have been taken from the facilities before but then again, I wasn't possibly expecting. There also wasn't any nanotech involved. Oh no. This could be bad. Maybe there is location assistance somewhere.

"How far are you ladies expecting to get?" A man with a black suit and brown shoes is walking towards us. Attractive. Blonde hair and blue eyes. There is a staff of four people navigating and driving.

"Julian, I just want to get her to an ultrasound machine."

I shoot a look over at Nature.

"No the hell you are not."

2

I don't know who these people are, but they can't just beam me up and do whatever they want to me. A woman in a red jumpsuit turns to me. It looks like she got a little too many "medical" upgrades to her face.

"Look, it doesn't work like that. I have a hierarchy. There are only certain places where we can do procedures and tests."

"Like that shithole we just rescued you from?" Julian snaps.

He has a good point. The facilities are pretty run down. What has my old man always said? Oh yeah, “the people who need the best of care get often times get the worst of care.” What can I say though, it's our cover.

Nature walks away with a phone call. And just like that, I am with a new crew. Let's wait and see what happens I guess. I take a seat on a leather bench. I'm starting to feel like a piece of property. I'm merely bouncing around like a ping pong ball. Why can't I go back to when times were easier? When it was just Jasiah and I? The world was so much easier to understand.

“Baby, chug your beer,” Jasiah looked at me playfully.

We stole a six pack of Heineken from his Dad's stash in the garage. It was our first night out since Baylor was born. We weren't old enough to drink so we were hiding out in an old casino parking lot. Laughing and giggling. I was getting wasted off of a beer and a half.

“Let's drink these and sneak into the back of the casino, I'm feeling lucky.”

“Oh are you now?”

A big smile crossed Jasiah's face. He wasn't even thinking about the possibilities. I was wearing a jean mini skirt and a blue tank top. Not to mention our tinted windows in the red Mustang.

I left my beer in the cup holder and squeezed into the backseat.

“Come on babe!”

Jasiah ripped off his Guess t-shirt and followed suit.

3

The jet jolts to a stop. The crew stays put while Nature walks back in from her phone call.

"Ms. Rayne, welcome to a real research facility."

I feel a little terrified. Where in the hell are we? I could use Max and his crew with the guns right about now.

"What exactly are we doing here?"

"Follow me Rayne, this is a place for women designed by women."

Since abortion legalization swept the nation, many centers had been opened to support women with reproduction, research, adoption and more.

The side door to the jet opens. We are directly up to the door of the facility. Bright lights and a medical crew meet us at the door. News travels fast. I must be famous in this place. I'm greeted by smiles and a wheel chair. And oh my god, Jolene! She slightly shakes her head and looks down as not to know me.

How did she get in this place? She is definitely here to support me; I can feel it. I sit down reluctantly into the wheel chair. I am whisked down a colorful hallway. Paintings of children and families line the walls. It lightens up the cold tile floors and teal walls.

I look back at the woman pushing me. Wrinkles line her face. She cracks a smile to expose a completely white smile but she has a gold incisor. A gold tooth. That is rare to see.

Very daring if her. Cross into the wrong neighborhood and that tooth is gone. Cross into a different neighborhood and organs will be even more valuable. This is uncomfortable to say the least. Being pushed by an elder. I should be pushing her. My mouth is dry and ashy. Ashes. Something isn't right. Why am I tasting ashes?

4

I'm not in control. I know that. But this is spiritual. Last time I tasted ashes, I literally became possessed and filled with rage. A language I had never spoken came flowing out. I ended up punching a hole through the wall. It scared Jasiah and my Mother into submission.

My ride ends in a sterile room with a metal examination table. My motherly instincts kick in. I don't want anyone in here to take what is inside my body if there is anything. I turn to see everyone in hospital scrubs and faces half covered.

“Rayne do you need help onto the table? We need to draw some blood and examine you.”

“I can do it myself.”

I might as well cooperate. First of all, I am outnumbered. Secondly, I want to figure out what's going on inside my body. At this point, I don't know who to trust. But between Nature and Jolene, I am feeling somewhat confident.

I lie on the exam table while a young woman attempts to check my vein for drawing blood. She reaches back and grabs a tray with her supplies.

“Make a fist dear.”

I ball up my fist and without warning, my skin and vein is pierced. I'm in awe. Out comes a bright red liquid with silver and white sparkles. I glance around the room to see some wide eyes. This is new. I've never seen my blood like this. It's always a dark red no matter what meds or treatments they give me.

"Oh this is going to be a fun night," the woman with the gold tooth smiles largely. Her eyes are lit up.

5

"Grab the ultrasound machine."

Maybe this will be a fun night. I always like being part of the research. This is typically the part where Max will offer me sleep meds. I can take them calmly or be given them by force. I voluntarily lift up my shirt.

My hands are sweating with anticipation. Jolene walks towards me with a pink liquid to rub on my stomach. She gives me a playful smile and a wink. This is going to be fun. I just wish Jasiah was here. Nature brings the wand close to me. Jolene winks at me again and rubs the thick liquid on my stomach. The wink. She never winks. Something more is going on here. I'm just going to trust her on this one. There is a reason she is here.

Nature touches the wand to my lower stomach. She turns the screen so that only her and her crew can see. She wrinkles up her forehead and frantically moves the wand back and forth. I want details. It's my body dammit.

What did or didn't she find? This typically isn't how my appointments from the past have gone.

“There's nothing there!” Nature shouts to the woman next to her.

I see a figure come to a running stop in the door frame. I feeling of relief washes through my body. It's Max. I'm safe. Whatever these people were planning isn't going to happen now.

Max rushes over to the table and grabs my hand.

“Are you okay?”

“As good as I can be.”

“Let's go Rayne, unless you want to stay.”

Jolene wipes off my stomach and lowers my shirt. I grab Max's hand and roll off of the table.

“You might want to move a little faster my love.”

Max picks me up in his arms and runs back through the door. We make it into the hallway and he turns to a sprint at full speed.

"Max I can," but I stop. There is no use. I need to be saved at this moment. I don't know my way around this facility. I have no idea where we are going. All I know is that I feel safe in Max's arms. Safer than I have ever felt.

He came for me. Why? He is always there for me. I hear the sound of bullets ricochet off of the walls. Max picks up the pace.

I can smell the night air. We are greeted by some men in uniform and a black SUV with an open door. Max throws me in the backseat and I tuck my legs underneath me. Max slams the backdoor and hops in the front.

“I'm so sorry for this Rayne. I have a lot of explaining to do.”

Max speeds out of the facility. Neither one of us look back.

“Thankfully Jolene has your back Rayne.”

“I can see that.”

“She saved your life back there and yours isn't the only one.”

Episode 12

1

“Rayne, I know about the bodies.”

“The bodies?”

“Not that you keep up with technology, but drones are getting pretty sophisticated.”

“I'm not sure I follow Max.”

“You are a killer Rayne! Just admit it!”

This isn't happening right now.

“Give me one good reason why I shouldn't send the feds to your hometown.”

“Why don't we go there together, I can see what you are talking about.”

Max reaches between his seat and the center console. Then he slams a beige file folder on my lap. I'm scared to see what's in here and how far he is going to take this. I flip open to the first page. The image sends me reeling to the past. The day my innocence was taken.

No, stolen. That bastard. I often try to forget but the nightmares won't let me. My subconscious won't let the evil memories fade. However, the man's face I'm staring at does not match the bones lying in my backyard.

I swore my secrecy to the man who knows who laid the bones there. I interviewed him in the prison before he died. When my father bought the home in two-thousand-eight, he wasn't totally aware of the history. However, after I was born, he found out way more than he wanted to.

The small house in Wisconsin was located in the quiet suburb of West Allis. The neighbors were friendly. My Dad was so excited because he got the home for way less than the asking price for other homes in the area. The area seemed safe, there were four seasons and the diners were fabulous. My molestation didn't happen there. Max has his timetable completely off.

2

“Max, this man has nothing to do with me, I promise.”

I'm going to leave Max confused, screw it. I was basically just born in West Allis; I wasn't raised there. Many years before we moved in, a man was murdered there. But the body was found. After the killer was caught, he gave up the location of other bodies. It looks like they missed one. Doesn't Max do his research? This was a high-profile case.

I know him better than this. He is trying to get me to out myself. He knows I didn't kill this man. He wants me to trip up. To get into the service, all of our records are searched through. Where we lived, where we went to school, all of it. But that was before Jolene. It looks like she is getting good at her hacking skills. No one knows about Memphis. Over a bottle of wine three years ago, we deleted the city I grew up in from my file. We stretched the West Allis timeline out to look like my family and I never moved. No one bothers to hunt down a paper trail anymore. But the man I am sitting with would. He has no problem taking it old school. And he is a very hard worker.

I don't feel comfortable lying to Max. But I am going to take my hunting days to the grave. Too many rapes and molestations happened back then. Everyone just turned a blind eye. Young girls would go on national television and cry their eyes out recalling what happened to them. It was the ultimate trigger for me. What happened to me was understandable and forgivable in comparison. I was in elementary school and my molester was in high school. But these girls? They were college-aged. I just couldn't wrap my head around it. These poor girls were getting treated like trash. Then they would put themselves on national television and pour their heart out to the world.

And what happened to the rapists? Practically nothing. Maybe probation or a few months in jail. But not to worry, I was waiting. I had some questions to ask them. I wanted to get their side of the story. At first it was harmless. A little torture, some hard questions. I did get my answers though. My face was always covered. I wore all black clothing. I was gaining the street name Cat Woman. It was invigorating. Intoxicating. I was becoming addicted to getting justice. Being feared. Typically, once I would have men subdued, they wouldn't fight it. Until one did.

3

One man said it was hot and asked if we were going to have sex. I lost it. It wasn't amusing and not at all funny. That's when I found out the truth about my heritage. Out came the fangs. I had no clue I had it in me. Without any warning to myself, I sank my teeth into the man's neck. All I saw was red. All of the anger and aggression brought out my animalistic nature. My Dad always joked about it. Supposedly I had asthma according to him. That is why he said I couldn't play aggressive sports. Also, he would always tell me to watch my anger.

"We don't want the fangs to come out," he would always say.

Well the fangs came out alright. There I was with my first dead body and no one to turn to. So, I went back to where it all started, the day I became a warrior. A crusader. The backwoods of Memphis, my real hometown.

I laid that man to rest right where I had punched a tree while my knuckles bled. He was my first victim. But he had created so many victims on his path to becoming a serial rapist. I did everyone a favor. I wiped that scum from the planet. I also stopped a lot of future destruction and heart ache.

4

What was I to do with my new found power? How much did my parents know? My Dad was always available to talk to me. My Mom was always too busy in the kitchen. She always avoided the hard questions. She never got too close to me. Anytime I would get upset or passionate about something, she would tell me not to get my blood pressure up.

Why would someone my age need to worry about that? It's like they were constantly planting seeds. Warning me. Well it would have been nice if they were more direct about it. I love my parents but come to find out, they kept me in the dark about a lot of things.

5

Jolene helped me turn up many redacted documents. It turns out the genes for becoming super human is present in many people's genetic code. For mostly everyone, those genes are deleted. But if a mutation on the deleted gene occurs, people like me can show traits of a million-year-old vampire. Myself and others have done a great job hiding ourselves for centuries.

Unfortunately, the government found a way to duplicate the traits. As well as capitalize, weaponize and of course monetize the duplication. But they needed blood. A lot of it. I had to be very careful not to be discovered. Just like any mutation of a deleted gene, I only show a percentage of the traits.

I don't turn to ashes in the sun, nor do I live for hundreds of years. But the rage met with angry fangs that can kill are fully there. Also, there is some strength beyond measure. Just like my PTSD, it has to be triggered. For me, the ultimate trigger is raping, molesting monsters. The men who have no respect for women. They take whatever they want and leave a trail of scars.

Max will never understand. Unless it happens to you, you can't fully understand.

"Women aren't the only ones who get sexually assaulted you know," Max gives me a long sad stare.

He took his eyes off of the road to tell me that. He never takes his eyes off of the road. It was genuine. Maybe he can relate. Poor Max.

He must've never told anyone. I want to ask a million questions but I don't want to pry.

6

I'm not quite sure where we are headed but it probably isn't good.

"Max where are we headed?"

"Where the hell do you think?"

Max grips the steering wheel hard.

"I can't have any more surprises Rayne."

"I'm confused. What surprises?"

"You are going to show me the rest of the bodies you hid out there in West Allis."

A laugh escapes my body. Does he realize we are about to hunt down a crime scene that is decades old? That murderous bastard ran rampant in Wisconsin decades before I was even born.

"Investigators are waiting for us there Rayne. Make sure you act innocent too."

This should be very interesting. Just wait until the forensic anthropologist steps in. Max will be very perplexed when he finds out the year the person died. And it has nothing to do with me.

"I'm good at pretending to be innocent," I shoot a flirtatious smile at Max.

Why not? I'm already in over my head. Might as well have fun with it.

7

Max shoots a look back. He smiles big and stares at me. There he goes, taking his eyes off of the road again. I turn and stare at the road for him. I hate not being in control. Let me drive dammit.

"You can tell me what's on your mind."

I already know this about Max. And that he is charming and good looking. He is also my boss.

"Thank you, sir."

"Don't sir me, you know me better than that."

Max turns my way again.

"Max, watch out!"

It's too late, a white compact car is headed straight for us. Max swerves to the right and off of the road. We plunge into the ditch and straight for a metal fence lined with huge trees.

Damn, this is how it ends? That's not going to happen. I love Max too much. I rip my seatbelt off and rip open the door and jump out.

Episode 13

1

Using all of my strength, I dig my feet into the ground. We stop just before the fence.

“Rayne! How in the hell did you do that?”

It's a long story. How do I explain that sort of strength? Max thinks he knows everything. But he doesn't know the half about me.

“Rayne! Are you okay?”

Max jumps out of the vehicle and runs around to me. Max grabs my upper arms.

“Rayne, you saved my life. How? And how do I thank you?”

“I had to Max, I um, I care for you very…”

Max leans in and kisses me with a force I have never felt before. My mind goes spinning. I lean back and stare into his eyes. As much as I may want to continue, I am very happily taken.

I reach back and slap Max with full force. His head turns and I can clearly see the hurt in his eyes.

“What the fuck did you think? I would just leave everything I've worked for in my life for you?”

“Whoa, whoa Rayne, it's not like that. I'm sorry, I let my emotions get the best of me.”

“Obviously,” I snap at him.

“Think of it as a kiss of gratitude.”

Max smiles at me gleefully. He is well, something. And his lips were very soft and alluring. He knows it too.

"You're welcome and I'm driving the rest of the way."

2

Max doesn't argue. I hop into the driver's side and press the engine button. I push the seat forward. Max is over six feet tall after all. Why did he have to kiss me like that? My head is full of mixed emotions. He and I have worked together for a while. We have grown closer by the day and he has always been there for me.

It doesn't change the facts though. I am taken. I have children.

"Ready Rayne? You can put it in auto drive."

"And how exactly does that work?"

"Well it's a little different than your Mustang that's over ten years old."

“Excuse me for being old school. Plus, I like a lot of muscle.”

“Oh do you now?”

I feel my face flush with red. I don't like the direction this is headed.

“Sorry Rayne.”

“It's okay, I'm used to the jokes from the guys.”

“Is that what I am to you Rayne? Just some guy?”

A feeling a guilt washes over me. Of course he's not just some guy. He means a lot to me. But I can't just sit here and pour my heart out to him. Besides, I am feeling extra emotional from our near-death experience. Max's earpiece lights up red.

"Max here." Max hops out of the SUV. "I'll be right back Rayne."

A private phone call. Could he be getting more information about a set of bones? Max paces in the grass and listens intently to the caller. It must be nice to have contact with the outside world.

3

A lot of people are getting permanent ear pieces installed to take calls and listen to music. I did a simulation for it and I just wasn't ready. Like I said, I'm old school. Besides, who needs constant communication anyways? I like to chat with the person right in front of me. And if there is no one there, well my own thoughts are fine.

"Rayne, come here for a second."

I hop out of the running vehicle and run to meet Max by the fence. He is pacing. He looks confused and angry. Aw, what's wrong? Didn't find what you were looking for? I should feel bad but I don't. Why was he so fast to criminalize me?

“Does the name Corey Beacon ring a bell?”

My face wrinkles with confusion. Who in the hell is that?

“Oh, I'm sorry Deacon, street name D.C.”

Oh now that sounds familiar. That asshole. Why the hell did he think he was God's gift? How could I forget? That skinny jean wearing, vaping, rapist. Once I got comfortable with killing, he was easy. Too easy. Especially since he was on the road to becoming a serial rapist. I am going to play dumb until I get more facts. For all I know, Max may be on my side.

"Who calls themselves D.C.? Sorry Max, you are on your own."

"Why are his bones buried behind your old home?"

"It's a setup Max or it was the new owner. I have no idea"

I don't want to ask him which home at this point. Either way, his body or what's left of him was moved at some point. Someone is fucking with me. My past is coming back to haunt me. In the worst way. I have no idea what to do or say or how to get out of this.

"Rayne! You're bleeding!"

Max points at my thighs. I glance down and then stare down. This can't be good. Max grabs me and scoops me up in his arms. Here we go again, my knight and shining armor.

"Come on Rayne, we are gonna get you to a real hospital." Max carries me to the door of his car. He opens the backseat and slides me in.

"Sit tight Rayne. I'm going to get you help."

4

Max hops in the front and speeds the SUV into reverse. I'm not feeling too confident but I'm in distress. A cramp that feels like my insides are getting crushed rips through my body.

"Max hurry!"

I'm feeling weak and faint. Please hurry Max. I hate feeling so helpless. What is going on inside my body? I close my eyes to see Jasiah. He is smiling from ear to ear.

"Come on baby, let's go!"

Jasiah and I ran, giggling into the old casino's back door. The janitor had left it open while he was taking the trash out. We just finished our beers and a very sweaty session of closeness in the backseat. It was invigorating. Empowering. I had gained my sexuality back. I felt like I could conquer the world.

Jasiah pulled out his wallet and opened it for me to see. There were over fifty bills of cash inside.

"Jasiah, where did you get that?"

"Don't worry baby, things are looking up, I promise."

Jasiah pulled out two twenties and handed them to me.

"Let's go!"

Jasiah grabbed my hand and ran to a slot machine. I was so buzzed and on cloud nine from our sexual session, I didn't even question it. I inserted a twenty and pulled down the lever. We laughed hysterically as we lost the forty dollars. We were so in love. Jasiah and I against the world.

"Come on baby, let's go, I gotta do a job."

It must have been the beer but I just decided to go with the flow. I trusted him. As we hopped in our sports car and drove off into the night, I had no idea what was in store for us. But my current pain level is surpassing that night.

Jasiah pulled up slowly down a dark street full of houses that were slightly unkempt. There were a few lights on.

"Wait here baby, this won't take long."

I didn't like it but I agreed. I trusted him. I always had. However, an uneasy feeling crept over me as Jasiah quietly moved down the street.

5

What is he doing for money? I thought to myself. Marijuana legalization was sweeping the nation so it might have something to do with that.

Jasiah ran back to the car at full speed. What the hell? There was blood dripping from his mouth. Two Nike duffle bags in his hands. Jasiah ran to the back of our Mustang and popped the trunk. Then, seconds later, it slammed shut.

Jasiah came to my side of the car and crumpled to the ground. I jumped out to see the most shocking thing of my life.

Jasiah shapeshifted into a beast I had never seen before right in front of my eyes. I wasn't the only one with supernatural secrets. Him and his family were keeping a lot of secrets from me.

My first thought was Baylor. He would have some highly sought-after genetic traits. Jasiah stayed there whimpering on the ground. I picked him up in my arms and we locked eyes. He had a look of fear and sorrow. Could I accept him this way? Then I noticed something missing.

6

His bracelet. He always wore an obsidian bracelet passed down through generations. He never took it off before. It was soldered shut. The bracelet was obviously something very special. I'd be damned if some asshole was just going to take it.

I lied Jasiah in his seat and leaned it back. He closed his eyes and drifted off. Something took all of his strength away. I was destined to find out who or what it was. I did have some strength of my own after all. It just hadn't been triggered in a while. I took off down the dark road.

Chills ran up my spine as I was running into the unknown. An older attractive woman met me at the end of a driveway. She had porcelain skin, jet black hair, a face of perfectly done makeup and a pit-bull by her side.

"You must be Rayne."

No shit lady. You don't know who you are fucking with, my body started to tense up.

"We were content with the bracelet as collateral, but we will take you too."

Episode 14

1

I submitted to the woman. Why not? I wanted answers to the mess I just inherited. These people somehow brought out the animal in my boyfriend. Literally. They may know his Achilles heel but I'd be damned if they knew mine. From the outside I looked like a harmless girl. I couldn't wait for them to trigger me. I had already taken down so many men a few years back. What was a few more?

Once I got into my studies, I had decided to hang up the towel of revenge. I wanted to figure out the why's of the human thoughts and actions. What dictated our behavior. How could a negative thought in our brain cause us to steal, rape or murder? Surely, these people weren't in the mood to learn about that.

I would have to resort to getting physical. But that was going to be my trump card.

"May I have my boyfriend's bracelet back? It's sort of a family heirloom."

"Sure young lady, right this way."

I followed the woman to an old gray house with vinyl siding. It was greeted by a wooden porch on the side. The pit-bull followed behind me. We walked into the side door. It was dark, marijuana smoke filled the air. I could smell beer that had been spilled a day or two ago. That's how it started; my sense of smell heightened. Then the goosebumps. Then I spotted the bracelet on a table next to a revolver, bags of cocaine and stacks of cash.

Not that easy. They would expect me to go for the bracelet. Instead, I reached for the revolver. Less about shooting and more about confusion. I took off the safety and shot the bags of cocaine. Powder filled the air. Not that I could see the men coming at me but I had my defense planned out. I could hear and smell them.

Using my hand with the gun, I blocked my first punch. I had no idea how many people were in the house or how many people would show up. I could feel the fangs about to come out. It was too late; my only choice was to kill. It was instinctual, they fucked with my man. And I had a strong feeling that he really needed that bracelet.

I wasn't sure if it was worth my life. The hits started flying in from three different directions. In the past, I had only fought one on one. feeling of dread washed over me.

"Take that bitch down!" The woman yelled from across the room. I grabbed the bracelet as a steel-like hand with a grip as tight as hand cuffs grabbed my wrist. Dammit.

2

"Take her downstairs!" The woman barked orders to the men. My eyes were burning. The room started to spin. Why didn't I just rush Jasiah to safety? What on earth was I thinking? I was brought down a set of basement stairs by a group of men that resembled bouncers at the local night club. My feet were barely touching the ground.

Luckily, I only used a fraction of my strength. I decided to keep my mouth shut and maybe gain some insight as to who the people were. From the sight of the basement, it looked as though I'd be forced to talk.

"Rayne! Rayne!" My body is being shaken. My jaw is clenched. I slowly open my eyes. My hero, Max. Max picks me up over his shoulder. Then he sets my body onto a cotton mattress. I stare up at the daytime sky. My stomach has turned into a storm. It feels as though there are lighting strikes ripping through my body. I see serious faces above me as bright lights hit my eyes. This feels familiar. A hospital. I'm scared. Confused. I need to see Jasiah. We don't always get what we want though. I have to be strong. From my pain level, I'm going to need surgery.

"Sir, you can't come the rest of the way."

"I'm not leaving her!" Max yells and flashes a badge in his wallet.

"You are to stand in the corner of the room and give us space sir."

“You got it nurse, thank you so much.”

Thank God for Max. I need a familiar face and voice. My stomach hurls in pain. We reach our destination room and everything just stops. People are scrambling around me and I am left in a fog. I can barely breath. I can't speak. My eyes close and I am left with my memories from the past. I return to the first night I came inches to losing my life and the beginning of all of this.

3

“We know what runs through your blood young lady,” a man with a weathered face hissed at me. He ran his hand through my hair as he sniffed the strands. I was repulsed by him. I tried to wriggle free but the thugs had me in their grasp.

“I can smell it in your pheromones. It oozes out. That is how we find each other. You are part of us now. You tried us. Welcome to Black Bones my lady.”

I wanted nothing more than to end him right then and there.

“Do you know how much cocaine you just wasted? You are going to have to work to pay that off. What kind if skills do you have?”

This asshole has to go down I thought to myself, I knew it was true. I just didn't know how. I wasn't part of Black Bones either. There was no way I was teaming up with a bunch of thugs.

“We've been watching you,” the man pulled me close and parted a smile of perfectly white teeth. He slowly took a hand of razor-sharp claw-like nails down my face.

"So pretty, so young."

I darted my eyes around the room. Definitely an atmosphere for cooking up drugs. Not very much visual or intellectual stimulation. But this guy was smart. He was losing his precious combed blonde hair by the day. But judging by the work done on his hand and teeth, he could pay to replace some hair.

4

"I served my time for our country," the man snarled.

"I've gone through every medical upgrade available. I'm unstoppable. Fake heart. Steal bones. You name it."

The man's breath smelled like whiskey and cigarettes. Was there a way to get on his good side? Reason with him?

"You think you are some bad woman? You have a bit of a body count so you think you can take me out? My crew?"

The man was making my skin crawl and my stomach turn. Also, I was feeling new symptoms. I could feel fire running through my veins. Whatever was going through my body was unstoppable. The man's fate was no longer in my control.

"Hickson."

"Hickson?"

"The last man you will ever lay eyes on."

Hickson took a balled-up fist and cocked way back. It hit my stomach like the force of a truck. The pain rocked my entire body. Shock waves shot from my stomach through to my limbs and back. The pain resonated straight to my brain. Dizziness started to take over.

Hickson let out an evil laugh, “We're just getting started!”

The men and woman in the room broke out in laughter with Hickson. The night was just getting started. My eyes glazed over and I let out a wicked laugh of my own.

Hickson backed up. The thugs looked confused. It pays to have a Daddy out in California, I thought to myself. He was the king of medical upgrades. We also had a basement like this growing up. We just weren't ignorant enough to drug deal petty cocaine and meth.

5

"What the fuck?" Hickson backed up further with his crew. I already knew what was happening. My Father did extensive research on gene splicing with animals as well as humans. What was happening was basically smoke in mirrors but it scared the hell out of those bastards.

My veins were slowly filling up with a black liquid. My Father was very interested in sea animals and their defense mechanisms. I was a good patient for him as a young girl and he paid well. It looked like I had come down with the plague. But that was just the beginning. His punch activated a lot of animalistic defense mechanisms. My Dad always chuckled and said we would slowly win the race to strength and power.

"Technology and fake body parts will only get them so far," he would always say. "It all boils down to genetics."

6

I was always mesmerized by the spinning DNA helix on his wall to wall screens. I put a hand on Mr. Hickson's shoulder and without a second thought, took his arm clean off. He let out the loudest scream I ever heard in my life. It resembled a three-year-old's shrill.

Next, I had plans to remove each pearly white veneer one by one. Footsteps stormed up the stairs. Good. Because that night, Hickson's body was so mutilated, in that basement, any serial killer from the past would blush.

It brought me back to my corner laboratory where Daddy worked. They had some rusty tools and chemicals to make it interesting. That man was a chump. It was funny how some upgrades made him feel so powerful. I always questioned my old man's motives for playing around with my blood. My Mom wasn't a fan but she stayed out of it.

"Honey, in today's world, a can of mace or even a gun isn't going to save you. You will thank me for this."

Oh I wanted to thank him alright. How many friends did Hickson have in the Black Bones gang anyway? I couldn't wait to test my strength again.

Episode 15

"I'm so sorry Rayne."

I open my eyes to see Jasiah.

"My baby, there was so much I didn't know. Max caught me up with everything."

I immediately panic. How much does Jasiah know? What did Max tell him?

"You are a hero Rayne."

I go to sit up but I can't. My legs are completely numb.

"Whoa baby, you just had major surgery."

Jasiah kisses my forehead.

"Are you ready to meet her?"

"Her?"

"The woman who saved your life."

I hear a light knock at the door.

"Hi stranger."

Jolene smiles from ear to ear. She has a handful of white daisies in her hand and a bottle of red wine.

"Well then," I gasp.

"We need to celebrate," says Jolene.

"Rayne, you had a lot going on in your body," Jasiah looks at me seriously.

That is an understatement. I can't believe I'm still alive. Max enters the room after Jolene. Three of my favorite people. However, it's awkward because they have all seen and know different sides of me. None of that matters now.

"Can I have the room you two?" Max asks in an authoritative tone.

Jasiah gives me a sweet, empathetic look. He leans down and kisses my forehead. Jolene sets her gifts on the table. She looks stunning in all black. Her favorite color. She is always in the background, saving my life in more ways than one. As they step out, Max has a seat next to my hospital bed.

"Hey there partner."

I look at Max confused.

2

"We have been put on a task force together."

Judging by the way I feel, I can't picture myself on a task force.

"Everything is out in the open now Rayne. No more sneaking into mental hospitals. No more using your PTSD as a cover."

"How did Jasiah take it?"

"Well, security had a field day holding him down and then cleaning up the broken furniture and glass in the waiting room."

I'm curious to know which side he showed Max.

"We could use him too on our team Rayne."

I look at Max very intrigued. I am not opposed to teaming up with Jasiah. However, him and I have a lot of emotional turmoil. I'm also wondering if Jasiah knows about the kiss between Max and I.

"I didn't exactly tell him everything Rayne. And I am sorry for what I put you through."

There was no need to apologize but his apology was sincere.

“It's Black Bones Rayne.”

The sound of that name makes me shudder. How could I forget? The gang who has never forgiven me for my actions against them. Jasiah still has no clue exactly what I did that night. From what I can tell, neither does Max.

“They are completely underground. They are exploiting, well, people like you and Jasiah. Horrific things are happening to them.

“People like me?”

“Don't play me Rayne. I saw you stop the car. And the blood tests don't lie. Jolene jumped through a bunch of hoops to get you a proper blood transfusion. It was quite the cocktail.”

“My Dad?”

"He was here too Rayne, we almost lost you."

"Where is he?"

"He is making sure we don't run into this problem again which is why we need him too. Hickson and his crew are synthesizing blood of people like you and Jasiah and it's not pretty."

"Hickson?"

"You've heard of him?"

"It rings a bell."

Apparently, I either killed the wrong Hickson or it's just a coincidence. I decide to keep that fact to myself. I have always been good at playing sweet and naïve with Jasiah. But now? How much does he know?

3

"The blood?"

"It was the remnants of some major experimentation inside of your body. Possibly a miscarriage with it. The doctors still aren't sure."

"You didn't think to start there?" My face flushes with anger.

"I'm not good at this type of thing Rayne. Plus, I blame myself. You saved my life."

"It's not your fault Max. Between the Microtech, the microbes and the drugs, it would have happened anyways."

"But still."

"Max." I stare deep into his eyes. He can't blame himself for it. But I can't stop the way he feels.

"Rayne, they are abducting children and doing horrific experiments on them."

My Achilles heel. Children. Where my emotions get the best of me.

"Looks like we have something bigger than us to worry about Max."

"We think that your children could be in danger. But we need you and Jasiah."

I don't want this to be true but it won't end until we end it. The real Hickson and his crew know who I am. How could they forget? The blood bath I left in that basement sent a message. I have always looked over my shoulder waiting for their revenge. But they have been playing the long game. Now my children are at risk.

4

"We will take them down one by one Max."

"I am glad you are in."

Max grabs my wrist. He cares about me and I care about him. Now we have a mission to care about together.

"Jolene?"

"She will be the brains of this operation."

"Looks like we have quite the team."

"Yes we do." Max winks at me, stands up and walks out of my hospital room.

I may not be able to avenge every death. I may never get my revenge against the person who stole my innocence. It's not that I can't wipe him out. I just can't get to him. If I tried to, I would lose everything. I would never get away with it. He's too high up in the government and too protected.

I will prowl A1A again. I will see his fortress. I will feel triggered to take his life. But I can't. I won't. He is protected by his title in the FBI. So, I will sit and dream of him being taken down. I can only imagine what he gets away with now. It was in his monstrous stare.

He enjoyed stealing joy and innocence. He took pleasure in the pain of others. It was deeply ingrained in his soul. No matter how much justice I seek, it will never take the pain away. Using my strength and power will never bring back my innocence or that of the young women who came after me.

So, I will do what I do best. I will become better. Faster. Stronger. I will hide my true colors and fit in where I can. I will pretend the hurt is gone. I am a survivor after all. I have felt so powerful until now. I am powerless. Hurt. Helpless. But not hopeless. There is a huge difference. Hope will always be there for me. It has to be. I am not a victim anymore.

Only a victim of my own mind. My dreams will always haunt me. The darkness will always remind me. I may feel like my brain is locked in a cage. But I must break free from the cycle of entrapment. From this day forward, I will use my powers for good. I have a team of people who know who I am. No more secrets. No more hiding. No more lies.

I must walk through the woods of Memphis again. Uncover the burial grounds of my wounds. Show the secret side of Rayne. The angel and the devil within. The Dark Angel.

Narcissistic Episode Series (Preview)

Amy Perez MS Psychology

Published 2019

ISBN: 9781795835602

Printed by Amazon

Front Cover Design by Author.

Book Design by Designer.

Author: Amy Perez MS Psychology

https://www.amazon.com/kindle-dbs/author/ref=dbs_P_W_auth?_encoding=UTF8&author=Amy%20Perez%20MS%20Psychology&searchAlias=digital-text&asin=B07H24NKYJ

Episode 1

1

"Baby! We have new neighbors! And they have kids!" He sure is handsome. My husband. I cannot believe we're married. What a dream come true.

"That's great sweetheart. Oliver will have someone to play with." Mitch grabs the chicken to put it on the grill. This is fancy compared to our usual hot dogs and hamburgers. I swear, I thought we were done being broke. Until Mitch took an internship.

"Baby can you grab the melted butter off of the counter?"

"Sure sweetie." I walk through the sliding glass door. Things will get better, they always do. I peak into the living room to see a zombie. At least that's what I call Oliver when he's engrossed in video games. He is staring the screen with his bright blue eyes. I glance at his blonde hair. It's getting kind of long. I guess I can charge a haircut on my credit card. Oh yeah, butter.

This is a special night. It's Friday. Typically, Mitch would be working nights and weekends in the service industry. But not anymore. He's an intern and he works normal hours. Thank God. This is all I've ever wanted. Oliver and I have spent so many nights, weekends and holidays alone. I walk through the door to see Mitch talking to a man. He is the definition of Caucasian.

He has light skin, blue eyes and dirty blonde hair. He is skinny but muscular. It is a vast difference against Mitch's dark features. Being Italian gives him an authentic look. The men look pretty infused in their conversation. I quietly walk up with the butter and set it on the grill.

2

Ah, the kickoff of spring. This winter was rough and freezing. That's how New York is though. But the city is gorgeous. You just have to take the good with the bad. My family is minutes away. The school systems are great. My husband and I are in great schools. Back to work for me.

I walk into the kitchen and adjust my mannequin. She is wearing a fashionable red top. I should make about fifteen dollars off of it. It isn't what I planned on doing for work. But I can't afford child care in the area. Plus, it keeps me busy. Not that I need it. Studying psychology is pretty tough. My neuropsychology class is kicking my ass.

I snap a few photographs of my mannequin. Hey money is money. It's not forever. Honestly, it's pretty enjoyable. I glare out of the door wall of our townhouse to see the men laughing. Looks like we will get along with our new neighbors. The smell coming in from the grill is intoxicating.

"Baby, come here for a sec." Mitch waves a hand.

3

I pull open the screen door. The screen is hanging off of the frame. The life of having a dog and a cat. I manage to crack a smile. What is it called smiling depression? A great way to hide the pain. I am really good at it. Mitch is able to see right through it though. I do enjoy that he can light a match in my darkness.

"Hi, how are you?" I give a nice smile. "My name is Noelle."

"Chance. Chance Robins."

"Nice to meet you Chance."

His eyes are crystal blue. They seem to pierce right through me.

"You are going to love this area. The school system is great for your children."

"Oh no, they aren't mine."

I stare at him blankly. I don't want to judge or make any cliché reactions. I don't exactly come from the most picture-perfect background myself.

4

"Can I grab you a beer Chance?"

"Sure, that'll be great."

I turn to walk away. That guy doesn't seem super respectful. His demeanor. He definitely feels superior, that is obvious. I grab a Bud Light out of the fridge.

This is the shittiest beer ever. At least for me. It's safe though. Everyone loves it. Should I shake it up? Knock him down a peg? I pulled the prank on my Grandfather when I was about seven. He wasn't too happy. Thank goodness he had a good sense of humor though. I'll play nice, for now. I gently twist the cap off and toss it on the counter.

"Oliver, dinner is almost ready," I call out to my little angel.

"Okay Daddy!" I check the boiling corn on the stove. It isn't quite time for sweet corn yet but it will be pretty good. I poke each corn on the cobb with a fork to get them to spin. Just about done.

I hear Mitch bust out laughing. I just want him to be happy. He deserves the world. Life isn't exactly easy at the moment. However, we are healthy and the weather is finally warm.

5

Personally, I love the snow. I love to play in it with Oliver. I love sipping coffee while watching the snow fall outside my window.

"Here baby."

Mitch reaches out a hand for the cold beer. I'll let Mitch handle Chance. I haven't made my mind up on him yet. Two blonde haired girls come running behind the row of townhouses. Their blonde curls are blowing in the breeze. How cute, I can see a resemblance.

So, what did Chance mean by the fact that they weren't his? Was he kidding? Are they adopted? Mitch and I adopted Oliver when he was a baby. We were so happy. The day that we got approved to be foster parents was the best day of our lives.

6

I don't want to be the nosey neighbor type though. That's not my style. Eventually, I will hear their story. I am really good at getting people to open up. It happens everywhere I go. People just end up telling me their whole life story.

I guess that's why I am in school to become a psychologist. I love to hear people's life story. Plus, I have a family history of mental illness. It just makes sense.

I turn the burner off and cover the corn. It just needs to sit for ten minutes and it'll be done. Mitch and Chance seem to be getting along great. Stop it Noelle. Don't be so jealous all of the time. I hate that about me.

7

That is my least favorite personality trait. I try so hard to hide it. I am always jealous of my sister too. It isn't because she is a woman. It's just that I feel like her and my Mom are closer than I am to them. I know it's dumb. I just can't stop it. It's just like I don't have the same connection. I do like some of the same things as they do. I just don't have enough time for shopping and going out like I used to. Oliver takes up all of my time.

I just love him, I really do. I just never feel like I am enough. I definitely took on the Mommy role right away. Hopefully he isn't confused by having two Dads. Hell, sometimes I'm confused.

What should Mitch and I each be responsible for?

I even get jealous if him and Oliver are closer than Oliver and I. Ugh, as much as I want to be a psychologist, I feel like I am the one who needs the help. I plop down on the couch next to Oliver and place my hand on his knee.

“Hey Buddy.”

Oliver gives me a glance. Then he stares back at the screen. My little zombie. Good thing he only gets an hour a day.

All of the sudden I hear shattering glass. What the hell? I jump up from the couch to check on Mitch. My fight or flight mode has been activated.

Episode 2

1

"Babe, he tripped!" Mitch yells from outside.

Chance stands up with a confident smile. Beer is covering his sliding glass door. I run over and grab a paper towel roll. A woman with blonde hair, tattoos and piercings comes around to the backyard. She is fairly straight-faced. She should seem more excited for just moving into a new place. I run over and reach the paper towel over the fence.

"Thanks man, I appreciate it."

"You're bleeding."

Chance looks down at his hand. He doesn't look phased. That's weird.

"Shit." Chance whips open his door and stomps inside.

Mitch grabs the chicken of off the grill as if nothing even happened. How can he be like that? He has such a lack of empathy. Especially for strangers. He seems to only genuinely care for Oliver and I.

He always seems very obsessed with me. He is overly involved in my life. If we get into an argument, he won't even let me walk away. He follows me. Honestly, he scares me sometimes.

He was ordered to take anger management classes when he was a teenager. If it wasn't for my Father, I would probably question him more. My Father loves him. He is always bragging about Mitch. He says that he gained another son the day we got married.

2

"Baby, you gonna help me out?" Mitch is slicing the chicken on a cutting board.

"Yes boss."

Mitch doesn't say anything. He typically doesn't reply to my sarcasm. I feel like one day, he is just going to snap.

I grab a pair of tongs and grab his butt with them. He gives me a side eye. I know he is stressed about the new job. I get it. I'm just trying to break the tension.

"Can you clean up those clothes and your mess?"

Damn. Okay. I wanted to work after dinner but Mr. Clean freak has other plans. He gets it from his Mother. I am a clean person, but damn. They want perfection. It is literally impossible to keep a house perfect. Especially with a young child. He is always experimenting and making messes.

I grab Sally to take her down to the basement. That's the name of my mannequin. My sister taught me to sell clothing online. I named my mannequin after the store that we buy clothing from to resell.

This basement gives me the creeps. It is cold and unfinished. All of the brick townhouses in our row have the same creepy basement. If one floods, then they all flood, it's the worst. I set Sally in the corner. I glance over at Mitch's technology bins. They are off limits to Oliver and I. Mitch is a huge video gamer. He goes live on the computer three times a week. He has gained thousands of followers this year. I am happy for him. And of course. Jealous.

"Babe!"

"Coming!"

I walk up the wooden basement stairs to darkness. What the heck? There are two candles lit on the table. Mitch is standing at the table with roses. I give him a surprised smile.

"They were in my car." Mitch hands me a card. He really is so sweet. I peel open the envelope. It's a thank you card. I start to read the inside. A tear falls from my cheek

3

How does he always do that? He always makes me cry. He is so sentimental.

"I love you." Mitch leans in for a kiss.

Our passion hasn't dwindled in our fifteen years together. We have been through so much and hard times. The worst was when I got diagnosed with manic depression. Even though it was devastating, it was a relief. We finally had an explanation for my behavior.

We found out why I would explode with anger and irritability. It explained my sleepless nights. No matter how bad it got,

Mitch stayed by my side. Literally, everyone in my life has either shied away or walked away. Except for Mitch.

We embrace each other in a long hug. Just what I needed.

"Baby, it's Chance."

Mitch backs away. "You're jealous of him?"

"No, it's Chance, he is staring in our window."

Mitch turns to look outside. Chance is standing by his fence glaring in our window.

"Maybe he likes red heads with green eyes." Mitch pokes me in the arm.

"So, not funny!"

"Fuck him, he's a weirdo babe."

How is Mitch like that? Literally, nothing phases him. I am officially creeped out. Does he have a problem with gay people? It wouldn't be the first time we have encountered it.

Oliver comes running into the kitchen.

"Yummy!" He shouts.

Mitch and I bust out laughing. Oliver is so dang cute. He keeps us on our toes, that's for sure.

4

Mitch pulls out a bottle of Meiomi Pinot Noir. It's the wine we bought the night we got engaged. Wow, he is pulling out all of the stops. Shit. He must have to go out of town. Dammit. His new job. He mentioned them having him go to Mexico. It's the worst. But the positive side is that he will bring in more money.

"So, when do you leave?"

Mitch let's out a sigh. "In the morning."

"It's okay, Oliver and I can hang out with my Dad."

"Okay my baby."

Mitch twists open the cap to the wine. The wine glasses are already on the table. Oliver is already digging into his chicken. Mitch put some melted butter in a dish on the side of his plate. Oliver sure is fancy. I don't exactly want to be left alone with the new neighbor.

5

He gives me the creeps. He seems like the guy that all of the girls drool over but deep down he is really a douche bag. Mitch pours our wine as I take my seat. I am just feeling so grateful for where we are in life. Life really is good.

"Oliver, sweetie, do you want some salt on your corn?"

"Yes please."

"Baby, I'm going live tonight."

"Of course you are, gotta give the followers some action." I give Mitch a playful wink and smile.

6

Ah, so perfect. I am loving this basement. At first, I thought I could use it to practice karate. But now I know of something better. For now, it will be the new home for my pieces. My puzzle pieces that is. I have built quite the collection. The taste of Jack Daniels and Coke crosses my lips. The sweet taste rolls off of my tongue. I am building the most beautiful sculpture. The female body.

It is going to be a masterpiece. It just takes time. My way of getting the pieces isn't exactly easy. The last one was the fight of my life. I turn on my computer to get started. My research.

Each candidate must be carefully planned out. The skin color must be perfect. These damn camera filters that the girls are using is making it difficult.

I don't mind the challenge though. I have already planned my next piece of my puzzle.

"Hello Jolene." A smile crosses my face. Why is this so exciting? Puzzles are just so exhilarating. Once you find the right piece, you can feel so relieved. The stress just melts away. I hear tiny footsteps upstairs. I better make this quick.